By Augusta Huiell Seaman

To my severest critic, my father, and to Virginia, who was its inspiration, I dedicate this book

Cover design by Tina DeKam
Cover illustration by Lydia Colburn
First published in 1910
This unabridged version has updated grammar and spelling.
©2019 Jenny Phillips
www.thegoodandthebeautiful.com

Introduction: Fair Leyden

I am glad that Mrs. Seaman has written this story. Americans cannot know Leyden too well, for no city in Europe so worthily deserves the name of Alma Mater. Here, after giving the world an inspiring example of heroism, modern liberty had her chosen home. The siege, so finely pictured in this story, took place about midway in time between two great events—the march of Alva the Spaniard and his terrible army of "Black Beards" into the Netherlands, and the Union of Utrecht, by which the seven states formed the Dutch Republic.

This new nation was based on the federal compact of a written constitution, under the red and white striped flag, in which each stripe represented a state. Under that flag, which we borrowed in 1775 and still keep, though we have added stars, universal common school education of all the children, in public schools sustained by taxation, and freedom of religion for all, was the rule. Leyden won her victory seven years before the Dutch Declaration of Independence in July 1581. As our own Benjamin Franklin declared, "In love of liberty and bravery in the defense of it, she (the Dutch Republic) has been our great example."

With freedom won, as so graphically portrayed in this story, Leyden enlarged her bounds and welcomed to residence and citizenship three companies of people who became pioneers of our American life. Like the carrier pigeons, they brought something with them. To our nation, they gave some of the noblest principles of the seven Dutch United States to help in making those thirteen of July 4, 1776, and the constitutional commonwealth of 1787, formed by "the people of the United States of America."

First of all to victorious Leyden came the Walloons, or refugees from Belgium, to gather strength before sailing in the good ship New Netherland, in 1623, to lay the foundations of the Empire State. Then followed the Pilgrim Fathers of New England. Many of the young and strong who sailed in the Speedwell and Mayflower were born in Leyden and spoke and wrote Dutch. The old folks, who could not cross the Atlantic, remained in Leyden until they died, and some were buried in St. Pancras and St. Peter's Church. In this city also dwelt the Huguenots in large numbers, many of whom came to America to add their gifts and graces to enrich our nation. Last, but not least, besides educating in her university hundreds of colonial Americans, including two sons of John Adams, one of whom, John Quincy Adams, became president of the United States, Leyden, in 1782, led in the movement to recognize us as an independent country. Then the Dutch lent us four million dollars, which paid off our starving Continentals. Principal and interest, repaid in 1808, amounting to fourteen million, were used to develop six thousand square miles of Western New York when New Amsterdam (later called Buffalo) was laid out, and whence came two of our presidents, Fillmore and Cleveland.

A most delightful romance is this of Mrs. Seaman. True to facts and exact in coloring, it is all the better for being the straightforward narrative of a real boy and a genuine girl. Gysbert Cornellisen's cooking pot, once smoking with savory Spanish stew or hodge-podge, is still to be seen in the Stedelyk (city) Museum, which every American ought to visit when in Leyden. It is in the old Laken Hal (or cloth hall). From the turreted battlements of Hengist Hill (Den Burg), we may still look out over the country. If in Leyden on October 3, one will see Thanksgiving Day celebrated, as I know it was, most gaily, in 1909, in a most delightfully Dutch way, when the brides of the year are in evidence. In Belfry Lane, where Jacqueline lived, was the later home of the Pilgrim Fathers.

On the wall of great Saint Peter's Church is a bronze tablet in honor of the pastor of the Mayflower company, and inside is the tomb of Jean Luzac, "Friend of Washington, Jefferson, and Adams." His newspaper, printed in Dutch and French during our Revolutionary War, won for us the recognition of three governments in Europe. On the Rapenburg, where he lived, a bronze tablet in his honor was unveiled to the singing of "The Star-Spangled Banner" on September 8, 1909.

Having spent weeks in Leyden during a dozen visits, I can testify to the general historical accuracy as well as to the throbbing human interest of this story of Jacqueline of the Carrier Pigeons. It will be sure to attract many a young traveler to Leyden.

William Elliot Griffis
Ithaca, NY, January 8, 1910

Table of Contents

I. On Hengist Hill 1
II. The King's Pardon 7
III. Gysbert Becomes a Jumper 13
IV. In the Camp of the Enemy 20
V. The Decision of Jacqueline 26
VI. The Coming of the First Pigeon 32
VII. A Swim in the Canal and What Came of It 38
VIII. "Tranquil amid Raging Billows" 44
IX. Vrouw Voorhaas's Secret 51
X. The Beggars of the Sea 56
XI. Jacqueline Responds to an Urgent Summons 62
XII. Reunited 68
XIII. Adrian Van der Werf 74
XIV. Alonzo de Rova Is as Good as His Word 80
XV. The Eavesdroppers and the Plot 85
XVI. When the Wind Changed 92
XVII. A Crash in the Night 99
XVIII. The Dawn of October Third 106
XIX. The Secret Out 113
XX. The Great Day 118

Chapter I

On Hengist Hill

The hush of a golden May afternoon lay on the peaceful, watery streets of Leyden. Just enough breeze circulated to rustle the leaves of the poplars, limes, and willows that arched the shaded canals. The city drowsed in its afternoon siesta, and few were about to notice the boy and girl making their way rapidly toward the middle of the town. Directly before them, the canal-interlaced streets and stone bridges gave place to a steep incline of ground rising to a considerable height. Its sides were clothed with groves of fruit trees, and from its summit frowned the moldering walls of some long-forsaken fortress. So old and deserted was this tower that a great clump of oak trees had grown up inside of it and overtopped its walls.

"Art thou tired, Gysbert?" asked the girl, a slim, golden-haired lass of seventeen, of her younger brother, a boy of little over fourteen years.

"No, Jacqueline, I am strong! A burden of this sort does not weary me!" answered the boy, and he stoutly took a fresh grip on some large, box-like object wrapped in a dark shawl that they carried between them.

Up the steep sides of the hill they toiled, now lost to sight in the grove of fruit trees, now emerging again near the grim walls of the old battlement. Panting for breath yet laughing gaily, they placed the burden on the ground and sat down beside it to rest and look about them. Before their eyes lay pictured the sparkling canal-streets of the city, beyond whose limits stretched the fair, fertile plains of Holland and in the dim distance the blue line of the boundless ocean. Gysbert's eyes grew misty with longing.

"Ah! If I had but brush and colors, I would paint this," he sighed. "I would paint it so that all the world would think they looked upon the very scene itself!"

"Some day thou shalt have them, Gysbert, if thou dost but possess thyself with patience," answered his sister, with the gentle yet authoritative air of her three years' seniority. "We will raise many pigeons and train them. Then, when the price we have obtained from them is sufficient, thou shalt buy an artist's outfit and paint to thy heart's content. Meantime thou must practice with thy charcoal and pencil and wait till the war is over."

Both sat silent for a while, each occupied with thoughts that were, in all probability, very similar. The little word "war" recalled to them memories, pictures, speculations, and fears, all very painful and puzzling. Neither one could remember the time when their peace-loving land of the Netherlands had been allowed to pursue its avocations unmolested by the terrible Spanish soldiery. From time immemorial had these fair provinces been tightly grasped in the clutch of Spain. Now at last they were awakening, rousing themselves from the long inaction, and striking the first bold blows for liberty from the relentless oppressor. Little did the children dream, as they sat looking out over the beautiful city, that this same year of 1574 and this same Leyden were to witness the great turning point of the struggle.

"Look, look, Jacqueline! There is the church of Saint Pancras, and there is our house in Belfry Lane. I can almost see Vrouw Voorhaas looking from the window! Come, let us set free the pigeons!" And Gysbert, all excitement, began to fumble with the wrappings of the bundle. Jacqueline rose, threw back the two golden braids that had fallen across her shoulders, and knelt down to superintend the work.

Very carefully they removed the dark shawl and laid it aside, disclosing a box roughly fashioned like a cage, containing four pigeons. The frightened birds fluttered about wildly for a moment, then settled down, cooing softly. When they had become accustomed to the daylight, Jacqueline opened one side of the box, thrust in her arm, and drew toward her a young pigeon of magnificent coloring, whose iridescent neck glittered as if hung with jewels. The girl cuddled the bird gently under her chin and with one finger stroked his handsome head.

"Let us send 'William of Orange' first," she said. "He is the finest, strongest, and wisest and will lead the way. I am glad we named him after our great leader."

"But the message!" Gysbert reminded her. "We must not forget that, or good Vrouw Voorhaas will never know whether he got back first or not. She cannot seem to remember one pigeon from another. Here, I will write it." He drew from his pocket a tiny scrap of paper on which he hastily scrawled, "'William of Orange' brings greetings to Vrouw Voorhaas from Jacqueline and Gysbert." This he wrapped about the leg of the bird and tied it with a string. "Now, let him go!" he cried.

Jacqueline stood up, lifted the bird in both hands, and with a swift, upward movement launched him into the air. The pigeon circled round and round for a moment, then mounted up into the sky with a curious spiral flight. When it was many feet above the children, it suddenly changed its tactics, spread its wings taut, and made straight in the direction of Saint Pancras spire and Belfry Lane.

"Bravo! Bravo!" they cried, watching intently till its sun-gilded wings had all but faded from sight. "'William of Orange' is a true carrier pigeon! Now for the rest!"

One after another they released the three remaining birds to whom they had given the names "Count Louis" and "Count John" after the great William of Nassau's two favorite brothers, and lastly "Admiral Boisot." It seemed to be a fancy of the children to call their pets after their famous generals and naval commanders.

"These are the finest pigeons we have raised," remarked Jacqueline as she shaded her eyes to watch their flight. "None of the others can compare with them, though all are good."

"Now we have twenty," added Gysbert, "and all have proved that they have the very best training. No pigeons in the city are like ours, not even old Jan Van Buskirk's. When shall we begin to hire them out as messengers, Jacqueline?"

"Perhaps there will be an opportunity soon," answered the girl. "Now that our city is no longer besieged, we may have to bide our time. But no one can tell what will happen next in these days. We must wait, Gysbert."

"Come, come! Let us be going," said her brother restlessly, "and see if they all get back safely, and whether 'William of Orange' was first."

"No, let us stay awhile," replied Jacqueline. "It is pleasant and cool up here, and the afternoon is long. Vrouw Voorhaas will let the birds in and tell us all about when they arrived. We may as well enjoy the day."

She reseated herself and gazed off toward the blue line of the ocean, shut out from the land by a series of dykes whose erection represented years of almost incredible labor. The river Rhine, making its way sluggishly to the sea—a very different Rhine from that of its earlier course through Germany—was almost choked off by the huge sand dunes through which it forced its discouraged path. The girl's thoughtful mood was infectious, and Gysbert, after rambling about idly for a time, came and settled himself at her side.

"'Tis a strange hill, this, is it not, Jacqueline, to be rising right in the middle of a city like Leyden? Why, there is nothing like it for miles upon miles in this flat country! How came it here, I wonder?"

"Father used to tell me," said the girl, "that some think it was the work of the Romans when they occupied the land many centuries ago, while more declare that it was raised by the Anglo-Saxon conqueror Hengist. That is why it is called 'Hengist Hill.'"

"How different it would have been for us if Father had lived!" exclaimed Gysbert, suddenly changing the subject. "It seems so long ago, and I was so young that I do not remember much about him. Tell me what thou knowest, Jacqueline. Thou art older and must remember him better."

"Yes, I was eleven," said Jacqueline with a dreamy look in her eyes, "and thou wast only eight when he went away, and we never saw him again. We had always lived in the city of Louvain, and Father was a professor of medicine in the big university there. Mother died when thou wast but a little baby. I can just remember her as tall and pale and golden-haired and very gentle. Good Vrouw Voorhaas always kept house for us, and we had a big house then—a grand house—and many servants.

"Father was so loving and so kind! He used to take me on his knee and tell me many tales of Holland and the former days. I liked best those about the beautiful Countess Jacqueline of Bavaria, after whom he said I was named, and of how good and beloved she was, and how much she suffered for her people.

"Then came the day when he disappeared—no one knew how or where for a while—till the news reached Vrouw Voorhaas that he had been captured by the cruel Duke of Alva and put to death. It was at the same time that the young Count de Buren, the eldest son of our great William of Orange, was kidnapped from the University where he was studying and taken a captive to Spain. We had little time to think of that outrage, so great was our grief for our dear father. Vrouw Voorhaas dismissed all the servants, closed the house and sold it, and we came to Leyden to live in the little house in Belfry Lane, where we have been ever since."

The boy listened spellbound, though the recital was evidently one that had been oft-repeated but had never lost its mystery and sorrowful charm.

"I was so little," he said at last, "I only remember our father as a tall man with gray hair and beard, and very blue, twinkling eyes. It is all like a dream to me! But is it not singular, Jacqueline, that Vrouw Voorhaas will never talk about him to us, nor answer any questions when we ask about him? And she has told us never to mention his name to others and has made us change our last name from Cornellisen to Coovenden. I wonder why!"

"It is very strange," agreed Jacqueline, shaking her head, "and I do not understand it myself. She told me once that I should know some day, and till then must never question her." But the restless spirit had again seized Gysbert, and he scrambled to his feet to make another tour around the old fortress. Suddenly the girl was startled by his loud, insistent shout:

"Jacqueline, Jacqueline! Come here! There is something very odd coming across the plains! Come quickly!" She rose and ran to the other side of the hill, where she found Gysbert shading his eyes with one hand. With the other he pointed to a thin, dark, undulating line moving slowly in the direction of the city, while here and there the sun caught a flash of blue and white, as from waving banners. Jacqueline's cheeks grew white.

"The Spaniards!" she breathed.

"The Spaniards indeed!" shouted Gysbert. "And coming to besiege the city once more, when we thought they had left us for good and all. In five hours at most, they will be here in front of the walls. We must run to warn the Burgomaster Van der Werf to strengthen the defenses and make all speed to close the gates. There is not a moment to lose! Come!"

And without another thought but for the safety of the beautiful city, the two children clasped hands and ran at top speed down the steep hillside in the direction of the great statehouse.

Chapter II

The King's Pardon

A week had passed, and Leyden lay encircled by the Spanish army in a state of close siege. Eight thousand troops under the Spanish commander Valdez surrounded the city, sixty-two redoubts had been raised to bombard its walls, and moreover, the number of the enemy was daily increasing.

But within the town were only a small corps of burgher guards and "freebooters" under the command of brave John Van der Does. Three sources alone supplied the reliance of the beleaguered city—their trust in God, the stout hearts and willing hands of the inhabitants, and the sleepless energy of Prince William of Orange, their heroic national commander.

Jacqueline stood in the dovecote one morning about eight days after the trip to Hengist Hill, feeding her little troop of carrier pigeons. Her golden hair fell over her shoulders in two shining braids, her eyes sparkled, and her cheeks glowed with the pleasure of her occupation. Upon her shoulders, her hands, and even her head perched the feathered pets, so tame that they fairly disputed among themselves for the privilege of her attention. The dovecote was a room on the top floor of the little house in Belfry Lane. The sun streamed in brightly through the large, open window, the walls were lined with boxes serving as nests, and every detail of the room was, through the untiring efforts of Jacqueline, as neat and immaculate as a new pin.

Suddenly the door opened and Gysbert, hatless and panting, stood on the threshold.

"Ah, Jacqueline!" he exclaimed with true artist's instinct. "What a beautiful picture thou dost make, standing there in the sunlight with the pigeons all around thee! Had I but time, I would bring my pencil and sketch thee just as thou art. But hurry, hurry! The Burgomaster Van der Werf is going to make a speech and read two proclamations from the steps of the statehouse. Everyone will be there. Come, we must get near the front!"

"Yes, yes!" echoed Jacqueline, as eager as the boy. "Close thou the door tightly, Gysbert, and we will hurry, that we may not miss a word. Ah, I hope that the good William the Silent has sent the city a message!"

Out into the street they sallied, mingling with the crowd that was surging toward the open square in front of the great statehouse. The bells of Saint Pancras sounded the signal for a public meeting, and one could read from each earnest, excited countenance the importance that was placed on being present in this crisis.

"Look!" cried Gysbert. "There is Jan Van Buskirk not far ahead. I thought he was too ill with lumbago to leave his bed! See how he hobbles along! Let us join him, Jacqueline." They ran ahead and caught up with the old man, who greeted them cheerily, in spite of the pains with which his poor, bent body was racked.

"Yes, I managed to crawl out of my bed," he assured them. "'Tis important that everyone should attend these meetings in such a pass as we are now. Think you we will hear word from William the Silent?"

"Aye, but I hope so, though I do not yet know certainly," answered the boy. "We have received no word from him since the siege began. Surely he will not desert us in this hour of need!"

"See, Gysbert!" whispered Jacqueline. "There is that evil-looking Dirk Willumhoog across the street. Do not let us get near him. His very appearance makes me shudder!" The girl shrank closer to her brother and old Jan.

"Surely thou art not afraid of him, Jacqueline!" said Gysbert scornfully. "'Tis true I detest him myself, but I fear him not. What harm can he do us?"

"I do not know," replied his sister, "but there is that in his look that makes me think he would harm us if he could!"

"Poof!" exclaimed Gysbert. "Did I not tell thee that he stopped me in the street one day and asked me who we were, and where we lived, and who took care of us? I reminded him that it was naught of his affairs, as far as I could see, and left him to scowl his ugly scowl as I walked away whistling."

But the crowd had swept Dirk Willumhoog from their sight, and in a few moments they found themselves in the great square surging with people, and as fortune would have it, almost directly in front of the imposing statehouse, from whose high, carved steps the proclamations were to be read. They were not a moment too soon and had but just pushed their way to the front, near a convenient wall against which Jan might lean, when Adrian Van der Werf, the dignified and honored burgomaster of the city, appeared on the stone steps high above the crowd. The universal babel of tongues immediately ceased, and the hush that followed was broken only by the occasional booming of the Spanish guns battering at the walls of the city. Then the burgomaster began to speak:

"Men and women of Leyden, I am here to read to you two proclamations—one from our beloved William the Silent, Prince of Orange-Nassau—" here he was interrupted by loud and prolonged cheers from the multitude, "—and one from His Majesty, King Philip the Second of Spain." The absolute and scornful silence with which the people received the last name was but a fitting indication of their hatred.

"I shall read the message from the Prince of Orange first." And while the people listened in eager, respectful silence, he repeated to them how their Prince and leader, whose headquarters were now at Delft and Rotterdam, sympathized with them sincerely in their fresh trouble, and how he deplored the fact that they had not followed his suggestion to lay in large stocks of provisions and fortify their city while there had been time in the months before the siege. The Prince reminded them that they were now about to contend not for themselves alone, but for all future generations of their beloved land. The eyes of the world were upon them. They would reap eternal glory if they exhibited a courage worthy of the cause of their liberty and religion. He implored them to hold out for three months, in which time he would surely devise means for their deliverance.

He warned them to take no heed of fair promises from the Spaniards if they would surrender the city, reminding them of how these same soldiers had behaved at the sieges of Naarden and Haarlem, when, in spite of their declaration to let the citizens go out in peace, they had rushed in and murdered everyone as soon as the gates were opened. Finally, he begged them to take a strict account of all the provisions in the city and be most saving and economical with food, lest it should fail them before the siege was raised. When the message was ended, the crowds cheered themselves hoarse, and when the burgomaster inquired what word they desired him to send the Prince, they shouted as with one voice:

"Tell him that while there is a living man left in the city, we will contend for our liberty and our religion!"

"And now," continued Adrian Van der Werf, "hear the proclamation of the King of Spain. He invites all his erring and repentant subjects in the Netherlands, and especially Leyden, to return to his service, and he will extend to them full forgiveness for all their crimes. He declares that if any will lay down their arms, surrender themselves, and become his loyal subjects once more, that they shall receive his pardon, and all shall be forgotten. He has authorized General Valdez to say that if the city will surrender at once, that the citizens shall be shown every mercy." No sooner had the burgomaster ceased to speak than old Jan Van Buskirk raised his voice:

"It is a trap! Believe not in it!"

"Yes, yes! It is a trap!" stormed the multitude. "We will have none of it! We will die to the last man before we will surrender!"

"What right has that wretch of a Spanish king to offer *us* pardon!" growled Gysbert to his sister and Jan. "*He* forgive us, indeed! And it is he that has been doing all the wrong and committing all the crimes. Many thanks to him, truly!"

"But what message is it your pleasure that I shall send in answer to this?" asked the burgomaster.

"Tell him," roared Jan, who seemed to have constituted himself spokesman for the people, "that the fowler plays sweet notes on his pipe while he spreads his net for the birds!"

"Aye, aye!" assented the crowd approvingly. "Tell him that!"

"'Tis a good answer," commented Van der Werf, "and I will send it as it stands. Now who will take advantage of this pardon for himself? Let any who may feel so inclined come forward at once, and they shall be sent out of the gates to go their chosen ways in peace."

Another tense silence ensued. Each person stood his own ground staunchly and watched for any sign of wavering in his neighbor. Presently from out of the crowd there pushed a stout old man who finally gained the open space before the burgomaster.

"I am a brewer of Utrecht," he announced. "I do not live in this city and have no desire to maintain the siege. I wish to take advantage of the king's pardon!"

"Be it as you wish, neighbor," answered Van der Werf. "Here are the necessary papers. You shall pass out unmolested at the opening of the gate." The man received the papers while the crowd looked on, muttering in contemptuous undertones.

"And I," declared another who had shoved his way to the front, "will also receive the pardon, if you please." Jacqueline grasped her brother's arm convulsively.

"Dirk Willumhoog!" he whistled softly. "The city will be well rid of him, to be sure, but what a coward!"

When the two men had been furnished with the proper credentials, the burgomaster commanded them to proceed at once to the principal city gate, where they would be dismissed to the Spanish army outside. But as they made their way down the wide

Breede Straat, the fury of the crowd broke loose.

"Shame! Shame!" hissed the following throng. "Shame on the cowards who desert their countrymen to join the despicable ranks of Spain! Thrice shame on their accursed heads!" Straight to the walls of the city the multitude pursued the fleeing men, now actually trembling for their lives. The two children and old Jan, caught in the swirling throngs, found themselves almost on the heels of the fugitives. Jan grunted and spluttered his disapproval, but Gysbert seemed fairly boiling over in his wrath, especially against Dirk Willumhoog.

The gate having been reached, it was opened but the smallest crack available by the guarding soldiers. The brewer from Utrecht squeezed his bulky form with difficulty through the narrow aperture, followed by the howls of the crowd. But Gysbert could contain himself no longer. Breaking away from his sister's grasp, he rushed up to the remaining fugitive and shouted in his face:

"Shame on thee, Dirk Willumhoog, for a dog of a coward! Shame! Shame!" The man turned on him with so savage a countenance that Jacqueline could not repress a frightened scream. The cry attracted the man's attention to her also.

"You shall rue this, you two!" he vociferated. "You shall rue this day forever—and for more reasons than you now think! You shall rue it!" And the closing gate shut his wicked features and his impotent rage from their sight.

Chapter III

Gysbert Becomes a Jumper

"Turn thy face a little more to the light, Jacqueline. I want to get a full profile."

In the little living room of the house in Belfry Lane sat the two children on an evening a month after the events of the last chapter. On one side of the table Vrouw Voorhaas bent over a huge pile of mending, casting an occasional loving and solicitous glance at her two charges, but otherwise quiet, silent and reserved. She was a woman of large, almost masculine proportions, and her muscular frame knew not the meaning of fatigue. Her features were plain and unprepossessing to a degree, but nevertheless grave and intelligent. She was rarely known to smile, and her manner was as that of one weighted down with a great responsibility. Gysbert frequently told his sister that Vrouw Voorhaas acted as though she had some dark secret on her mind, and Jacqueline was forced to admit the truth of the remark. Her devotion to the children was beyond question, yet she seldom exhibited any outward expression of affection.

Jacqueline bent over a musty-looking old book, turning its pages thoughtfully and drawing her pretty brows together with a puzzled expression at frequent intervals. Gysbert sat on the opposite side of the table with pencil and paper before him, making a sketch of his sister's head as she leaned over her book.

"What is it thou art reading so intently?" he demanded at length.

"'Tis an old volume that belonged to Father's library—the only book that was not sold before we left Louvain," answered Jacqueline. Neither she nor Gysbert noticed the startled glance with which Vrouw Voorhaas raised her head at these words. Jacqueline continued:

"It seems to be all about medicine. Thou knowest how that subject interests me, Gysbert. I long, when I grow up, to practice the healing art. I feel in some way as if the gift were in me."

"Poof!" said the boy. "Women are not fashioned to be physicians—they have other duties! Thou art mad, Jacqueline! Such business is not for thee!"

"Ah! I know it is not considered a woman's business, and few if any have tried it. Yet there is the famous Queen Marguerite of Navarre. They say she is the wisest woman in France, for all she is so young, and knows not only Latin, Greek, and other languages, but much about medicine and the healing art also! I have been reading in this old book, but I can make little out of it, for there is much Latin in it, of which I understand nothing. But it is my great hope that someday I shall study all about it, even though I never become a physician."

While they were talking, Vrouw Voorhaas gathered up her work and without a word, left the room. No sooner had she gone than Gysbert leaned across the table and spoke to his sister in a voice scarcely above a whisper:

"Jacqueline, now that Vrouw Voorhaas is out of the way, I want to tell thee several things, some of which I learned today. One thing I have fully made up my mind to do—I am going to become a 'jumper'!"

"A 'jumper,' Gysbert! And what may that be?"

"Why, I might as well begin at the beginning and explain it all," he answered. "Thou knowest the siege has lasted now for over a month, and things are beginning to look black for us. There is no more bread in the city and but very little of the malt-cakes on which we are all now living. Precious glad I am that we were fortunate enough to lay in an extra stock of seeds for our pigeons, or we should soon be reduced to feeding on them!

"Well, I was in the square before the statehouse this morning, and through listening to and taking part in some of the gossip there, I learned a few things. In the first place, our good William the Silent cannot possibly raise a sufficient army to encounter the besieging troops of the Spaniards, that's plain. Relief must come in some other way, but how, God alone knows! However, our wonderful Prince is wise and resourceful. Let us not despair, but trust him to save us and do our best to help.

"Jacqueline, I am going to do *my* part! Tomorrow I go to Burgomaster Van der Werf to offer myself as a 'jumper.' Let me tell thee what that means. The Prince wants a few swift, skillful messengers who will go out of the gates secretly, in some kind of disguise, and make their way through the Spanish forces to him. Now I am young, I know, but I am big and strong, and I know my way around the walls and outside the city as well and perhaps better than anyone in Leyden. And I want to *do* something! I can't sit around idle while all are helping in one way or another. Why dost thou look so white and frightened, Jacqueline?"

"Ah, Gysbert! Thou must *not* do this! Thou wilt surely be captured and killed. Ah! I cannot allow it, nor will Vrouw Voorhaas!"

"Vrouw Voorhaas must not know of it—at least at first. And thou must not interfere with me, dear sister. I know that our father, were he alive, would approve of my decision. Did he not always tell us to be courageous, and would he not wish us to serve our city in this great distress?" This argument silenced Jacqueline's remonstrances.

"Do what thou wilt, Gysbert, since thou thinkest that our father would approve, only be not rash, and have a care for thy life. What would I do if thou wert taken from me, brother?"

"I will be most cautious, sister, never fear for that!"

"But how shall we keep it from Vrouw Voorhaas? She would lock thee in a room and never let thee out did she but dream of thy decision!"

"Thou mayst tell her that I am out helping with the defense

of the city if I fail to come back for too long a period. That will be the strict truth, yet not enough to alarm her seriously," answered Gysbert.

"How absurdly worried and careful she has been about us since the day we told her of the king's pardon and Dirk Willumhoog! She turned deathly white at the mention of his name, and I thought she was going to faint when we told her what he said before he left the gate. Dost thou remember, Gysbert?"

"Aye, but let me tell thee something else, Jacqueline. What dost thou think of this? I saw Dirk Willumhoog in the city this morning!"

"Gysbert! Thou art surely joking! That cannot be possible. Since he was expelled from the city, how could he get back?"

"Ask me not how he got back, for I do not know. But the best of it is that he did not see me, and he was so disguised that had it not been for certain circumstances, I should never have known him. I had strolled up Hengist Hill after leaving the Breede Straat and had climbed into a tree to get a better view of the Spanish army outside the walls. I was sitting in the branches very quietly when a man in a long cloak and big, slouching hat came out of the grove and sat down right under my tree. Thinking himself alone, he took off his hat, threw aside his cloak, and then to my great surprise, pulled off the thick beard that covered his face!

"'Ah, but it is hot!' I heard him mutter. Then he stood up and stretched his arms, and I all but lost my hold and fell out of the tree when I recognized who it was! He sat down again and rested for half an hour, and I thought he would never go. Fortunately, he did not once think of looking up or he would have certainly seen me. At last he donned his beard, hat, and cloak and sneaked off, never dreaming who had watched his every movement! I would give a good round florin to know what he is after!"

"Ah, I am sure it is some harm to us he is plotting!" shuddered Jacqueline. "Dost thou recall his look of hate on that dreadful day, Gysbert? He has some reason for wishing us evil."

"That may or may not be," answered Gysbert. "At any rate, I

think he can do us but little harm. However, thou shouldst be careful about going abroad in the city alone, Jacqueline. Thou art not as strong as I."

"I go nowhere except to purchase our small allowance of food—thou knowest Vrouw Voorhaas never goes out at all now—and to visit poor Jan Van Buskirk once a day and take him some soothing medicine. He says that nothing helps him like the decoction of my herbs, and nothing charms away his pain like the touch of my hands. Dost thou know, Gysbert, that he has been obliged to kill and eat most of his pigeons since food has been so short? I know not what he will do when they are gone!"

"We will share our food with him, Jacqueline. He has always been so kind to us and taught us how to raise and train our pigeons. But now, let us to rest! It is late, and I must see Burgomaster Van der Werf early tomorrow."

Poor Jacqueline's sleep that night was restless and tormented by frightful dreams in which Gysbert's new and dangerous vocation and the evil face of Dirk Willumhoog bore no inconspicuous part. Gysbert, on the contrary, slept sweetly and undisturbed as a year-old baby and rose next morning betimes to seek what fortune he should meet in this new enterprise.

Adrian Van der Werf sat alone in his great office in the statehouse. His fine face was clouded with an expression of intense gloom, and he shook his head gravely as he looked out over the besieged city. Was this fair spot to fall a prey to Spanish vengeance, as its sister cities had fallen? He saw no hope in present prospects for a better fate. Presently an official opened the door and saluted him:

"A small boy outside wishes to speak with Your Worship."

"Admit him," answered the burgomaster. "I am not engaged at present." Glancing up as Gysbert entered, his face lighted with a smile of recognition.

"Ah! Thou art the boy who warned us of the approach of the Spaniards! Thou art a brave and thoughtful lad. What can I do for thee?"

"Your Worship, I have a request to make," answered Gysbert

promptly. "I wish to serve my city by becoming a jumper!"

"A jumper—*thou*! But thou art scarce fourteen years of age, if I judge rightly. It would be wicked to expose one so young to such dangers!" exclaimed the astonished burgomaster.

"Aye, Your Worship, you have guessed my age correctly. But I am strong and agile and know the walls and outlying districts well. Moreover, I have a plan that I trust will take me safely through the Spanish lines."

"And what may be that plan?" demanded Van der Werf, more and more amazed.

"This," answered the boy. "I shall stain my skin and hair darker with walnut juice, that I may not be recognized. And pretending to be somewhat half-witted, I shall go out among the Spanish troops peddling healing herbs. My sister raises many such in her little garden and has taught me much of their use. In this way I can most likely get through the lines, unsuspected and unmolested, and deliver any message to your faithful ones who are beyond."

"It is a clever scheme!" admitted the wondering burgomaster. "And if thou dost act thy part well, thou wilt be fairly safe."

"Likewise," added Gysbert, "I have some carrier pigeons that have been exceedingly well-trained and perchance could make them of use also."

"The very thing!" exclaimed Van der Werf. "Our stock of carrier pigeons waxes very low, having either died of starvation or been eaten. I have been wondering where I should find well-fed, well-trained birds to fill their place. Canst thou take a couple at a time with thee? I must needs send some to William the Silent at Delft, else we will get no more messages from him."

"Aye, I can bind two and take them at the bottom of my bag of herbs," answered Gysbert. "I will wager for it that they shall be delivered safely."

Adrian Van der Werf spent a moment in silent consideration. "Thou art a brave and clever youth," he said. "But thou must know that thou art risking much in this hazardous enterprise. However, God will watch over those who serve Him. Come to me tomorrow bringing two carrier pigeons, and I will instruct thee as to the message." And Gysbert, highly pleased, departed for Belfry Lane, whistling lustily one of the popular songs of the day:

"Beat the drums gaily,
Bub-dub a dub-dee!
Beat the drums gaily,
And the Spaniards will flee!"

Chapter IV

In the Camp of the Enemy

In the cold, gray mist of earliest dawn, Gysbert crept silently through one of the city gates. So changed was his appearance that his own sister would scarcely have known him had she not assisted in effecting his disguise late the night before. His straight light hair had assumed a dark brown color, and his fresh, rosy complexion had suddenly become as swarthy as any Spaniard's. His Dutch blouse, cap, and wooden sabots were exchanged for garments of a more foreign cut, and in his hand he bore a large bag of assorted herbs, both green and dried.

Thanks to an almost daily study of the Spanish camp from his perch on Hengist Hill, he had selected the most favorable quarter for his egress through the enemies' ranks—the situation farthest removed from the headquarters of commander Valdez.

The camp had very much the appearance of a little city of mushroom growth—rows upon rows of tents, and here and there a hut of larger proportions hastily constructed of boards. In the middle of one tented street had been erected a rude shrine protected by an awning, at which knelt a priest celebrating the early morning mass. The tinkle of the silver bell calling to service was the only sound that broke the silence. Gysbert proceeded cautiously, rejoicing at every step that took him unmolested on his way, when suddenly a rough command arrested his progress:

"Halt! The password! What art thou doing here?"

"*Requesens!*" answered Gysbert glibly, thanking his stars that the burgomaster had not failed to inform him of the Spanish password for the day. Van der Werf had two or three trusted spies in the Spanish army who kept him well posted as to their daily plans and watchwords.

"*Requesens* is correct enough," replied the sentinel, "but who art thou, and where art thou going so early?"

"I am a Glipper," answered Gysbert in a sing-song nasal voice. "I come from the city. We are starving there. I sell these healing herbs in order to get some food." Now a Glipper was the name given to any Hollander who sympathized with Spain, and they were as a rule very favorably regarded by the Spaniards. Gysbert, being naturally truthful, disliked exceedingly to thus falsify himself but consoled his conscience with the motto, "All's fair in war." The sentinel looked him over suspiciously but concluded that he had not the appearance of a genuine, out-and-out Dutch boy. Moreover, it was evident from his speech and expression that he was not blessed with more than half the usual quantity of wits.

"Well, little fool, I will let thee pass, provided thou wilt supply me with something healing for this wound in my hand where the gunpowder from my musket burned me yesterday morn." Gysbert hunted in his bag, brought out a small bundle of dried leaves, and recited as if by rote:

"Thou shalt steep these in boiling water. Thou shalt make a poultice with the leaves thus steeped. Thou shalt bind it on thy wound. In two days thou shalt be better."

"Thanks, little fellow! Thy poultice and not thy wits have saved thee! And now, cut away quickly!" Availing himself not too hastily of the permission, Gysbert strolled away as if there were not a thought of danger in his mind. But no sooner was he out of sight of the sentinel than he took to his heels and ran swiftly and silently through the still-sleeping camp.

"If only I can reach the outskirts before they waken, all will be well!" he thought. Once again, only at the edge of the encampment, he was challenged by another sentry. But the password given, he was allowed to go on without question by a sentinel whose one sleepy thought was the bed into which he hoped soon to turn. Once on the high road to Delft, Gysbert's troubles were for the time over, and he abandoned himself to a leisurely walk and to the enjoyment of his breakfast, a stale malt-cake which he munched contentedly as he trudged along.

Then the sun rose, the morning mist evaporated, and the waters of the canal sparkled like jewels in the clear air of the July day. A lazy boat with one big brown sail edged its way slowly along the canal in the direction of Delft.

"I might as well save my strength," argued Gysbert to himself, "and what is more, I have time in quantities to spare. Hi! Herr Captain, I pray you take me on your gallant bark!" The captain looked up from a sail he was mending and scanned the boy from head to foot.

"I like thee not," he answered. "Thou hast too much of the Spaniard about thee, little frog! Thine own two good feet can carry thee!" Gysbert was secretly delighted that his disguise was so effective but hastened to add:

"Good Herr Captain, you are much mistaken. Look you!" And from the bottom of his bag he pulled out two pigeons bound and helpless.

"These be carriers!" he announced. "I am commissioned by Burgomaster Van der Werf to take them to our Prince at Delft. Also I have a message, but that is in my mind." Instantly the captain's surly manner changed.

"Come aboard! Come thou aboard!" he called heartily. "Thou art a small lad but a clever one. Here, catch this plank!" In two minutes Gysbert, comfortably ensconced in the stern, had curled himself up to finish the morning nap with which his early expedition had seriously interfered. In due time this easy-going vessel reached the Gate St. Catherine, the principal entrance to Delft, and Gysbert, disembarking, thanked the good-natured captain for his assistance.

"No thanks to me, youngster," replied the man. "It's all for the good cause, and my name is Joris Fruytiers, shouldst thou ever meet me and need my help again."

Gysbert set off with all speed to the *Prinsenhof*, the palace where William the Silent held his headquarters. One of the boy's greatest desires in life was to see and speak with this great father of his country, the Prince of Orange, who had been for several years his hero and idol. Hence his errand was all the more delightful to him since it was to afford him this coveted opportunity.

But this time he was doomed to disappointment. The Prince was away at Rotterdam, and his commissioner, Paul Buys, took the message in his stead. It was to the effect that the people of Leyden implored immediate help. They were on the point of facing starvation and feared lest the weaker ones would lose courage and yield up the city. Paul Buys sent word back to Van der Werf that the Prince of Orange was on the point of putting into execution a scheme of release that he had long been considering and would send word by one of the carrier pigeons when he was ready to put it into effect.

Buys then told Gysbert that hereafter he would not have to come as far as Delft with the pigeons but could leave them at the farmhouse of Julius Van Shaick, not far beyond Leyden, from whence they would be conveyed to Delft in safety. Before the boy left for his homeward journey, Buys superintended him in the disposal of such a meal as he had not seen for many a long day, and he sighed only that he could not convey some of it to Jacqueline and Vrouw Voorhaas.

Trusting to no slow-moving canal vessel, but relying mainly on the swiftness of his strong young legs, he accomplished the fifteen miles back to Leyden in four hours, and at nightfall reached once more the outskirts of the Spanish camp. But his passage through the enemy's midst was not destined to be as uneventful as that of the morning.

The camp streets were bustling with life and activity. Soldiers promenaded up and down, women—the few who had chosen to follow their husbands' fortunes—called to each other shrilly from the tent-doors, and even some children ran hither and thither in garments of startling untidiness. Gysbert hoped to escape notice in the general confusion, but in this he was mistaken. A sudden hand was laid in no gentle manner on his shoulder, and a voice from behind demanded:

"The password!"

"*Requesens!*" he replied confidently.

"In that thou art much in error!" answered the soldier. "Dost thou think that the password does not change from day to day? Thou art twelve hours too late. Come thou with me!" And he led Gysbert to the door of a tent which was empty and lighted only by a large fire outside.

"Here, Alonzo de Rova!" he called to a burly sentinel. "Guard this young interloper till I have time to report him to Commander Valdez."

"Now," thought Gysbert, "I *am* caught in earnest! But without seeming to possess any wits, I will try to use those the good God has given me as skillfully as I can." Alonzo de Rova paced up and down before the tent door for a time, apparently utterly ignoring the boy, yet in reality watching him keenly.

Gysbert on his part kept his eyes well open, yet assumed the vacant gaze he had attempted in the morning. Presently he took up a charred stick from the fire that happened to lie near him, and with it commenced to make some strokes on the white canvas of the tent.

"What art thou doing?" demanded de Rova, and he drew near curiously to examine the marks.

"Why, by the Pope!" he exclaimed. "It is myself—my very self as I stand here with my musket! Thou canst indeed draw, little stranger! Who art thou?"

"I am a Glipper," repeated Gysbert monotonously. "I sell healing herbs. I also can draw."

"Art thou indeed a Glipper? Well, that is not so bad! And look thou here! Canst draw a good portrait of me on fine paper?"

"Aye, I can!" answered Gysbert in his adopted nasal tone.

"Well, thou hast evidently not all the wits that God usually gives us, but thou shalt try," said de Rova, and he drew from his belongings a sheet of paper and what stood for a pencil in those days.

"Draw me well, little Glipper! Make of me a fine figure, for I wish to send it to my sweetheart in Madrid, and we will see what can be done for thee!" Drawing himself up to his full height, he assumed a martial position, ready for the likeness. He was truly a splendid specimen of a soldier and evidently very proud of his magnificent proportions. Gysbert seized the pencil and paper and went to work with a will. Never had he striven so hard to give satisfaction, never had so much been at stake, never had his art stood him in such good stead. When the picture was finished, Alonzo de Rova was profuse in expressing his wonder and delight and slipped a coin into the boy's hand.

"And now, little artist, fly! Slip away under the back of the tent when I am not looking and no one will be the wiser. The captain who caught thee is a good friend of mine, and beside, I will tell him thou art a Glipper. Remember Alonzo de Rova, and if thou dost ever come to the camp again, I will put thee in the way of earning a pretty penny, for there are many like me who would gladly sit for their portraits. I doubt not but that thou couldst make a florin a day at that work. One more word of advice—the password for tonight is *Philip*. Farewell!" With that he turned his back on the boy and commenced pacing up and down before the fire.

Gysbert lost not a moment's time, but acting on the friendly soldier's suggestion slipped out through a loose flap at the back of the tent. Thanks to the now dense darkness and his knowledge of the password, he escaped safely through the camp to the Cow Gate, where, giving a peculiar knock previously concerted between himself and the gatekeeper, he once more stood secure within the city walls. Speeding homeward to Belfry Lane, he murmured to himself:

"I have accomplished the mission without mishap and have also made two friends. On the whole, I think I have not done so badly!"

Chapter V

The Decision of Jacqueline

On the morning of Gysbert's first venture into the midst of the enemy, Jacqueline rose with a very heavy heart. She helped her brother with the last preparations for his departure; aided him in escaping the vigilant eye of Vrouw Voorhaas, who was already at work though the hour was so early; and bade him a tearful farewell as he sped down the silent street. But her mind was full of foreboding, and she felt as though she could never live through the time till he should return in safety. To pass the weary hours and otherwise occupy her thoughts, she assisted Vrouw Voorhaas with the daily routine of housework, cleaned the pigeon-house, and fed her eighteen remaining pets with a scanty supply of their rapidly diminishing stock of corn.

Vrouw Voorhaas had many questions to ask concerning the whereabouts of Gysbert, whom she had not seen that day. Jacqueline parried these as best she could, explaining that he had gone off early to execute some errands for Burgomaster Van der Werf. Her companion, unconvinced that all was as it should be and vaguely uneasy about her youngest charge, accepted the explanation somewhat distrustfully. To change the subject, Jacqueline began to talk about their supply of food and to make plans for husbanding it to the last crumb. While she was talking, her gaze suddenly riveted itself on the tall form of the older woman.

"Why Vrouw Voorhaas," she exclaimed, "how thin thou art

growing! See, thy dress dost hang about thee in great folds, and thine arms almost show the bones! Surely we have not yet come to the pass when such loss of flesh would be noticeable! What hast thou been doing?"

"Nothing, nothing, child!" exclaimed the woman hastily. "I eat as heartily as our supply of food will permit, but the hot weather always did reduce my flesh. Hurry away now, and see what thou canst purchase at the market, but try not to be seen too prominently. Young people are not too safe in the streets in these wild times. Art thou going to visit old Jan today?"

"Yes," answered Jacqueline. "He grows worse and worse, though I do my best to aid him. There seems to be something else ailing him beside just his lumbago, but I cannot quite make out what it is, and he will not see a physician. I will go out and gather some fresh herbs now to take with me."

The girl took her little basket and went out to her patch of garden at the back of the house. Gay flowers bloomed in one half of it, but the other was devoted to the cultivation of the medicinal herbs whose healing properties she had carefully studied in the old book belonging to her father. First she gathered a sweet-smelling bouquet of late roses and jasmine to cheer the eyes of old Jan, and then stooping among the herbs selected those most calculated to help his poor infirm body. When this was done she re-entered the house, added some malt-cakes and a bottle of Vrouw Voorhaas's cooling homemade wine, and proceeded on her errand of comfort.

Jan Van Buskirk's home was on a tiny street just off the Marendorfstrasse, and to reach it Jacqueline was obliged to take a rather circuitous route that led through the poorest section of the city. What she saw there on that day tore her gentle heart with an agony of sympathy. The weather was extremely hot and oppressive, and everyone seemed to have sought the coolness of the shaded street in preference to the little suffocating rooms. Pale, emaciated children thronged the doorways, many gnawing on dry, unsightly bones from which the last vestige of meat had long since disappeared. Sick babies wailed fretfully while haggard men and women strove in vain to comfort them. And here and there lay, stretched on an improvised cot, the form of some person desperately ill, moaning piteously. Jacqueline contrasted the scene with these same comfortable, happy people of a few months before, and her heart grew rebellious at the mighty suffering entailed in just the little word "war." "Is there no help—no help for it?" she asked herself.

Jan Van Buskirk was worse, unquestionably worse than when she had visited him before, and his condition alarmed her seriously. He was tossing from side to side, rolling his head feverishly, and muttering incoherent words; nor did he seem in the least to recognize his little friend. Jacqueline quietly determined that it was high time he had more expert medical advice than she could offer and went out hastily to seek the nearest physician. Dr. Pieter de Witt was hard to find, for his duties were long and arduous in these dreadful days, but finally she discovered him in the house of a poor family all sick but the mother, who could hardly drag herself around. Hearing Jacqueline's errand, he made haste to accompany her. One glance at the unconscious Jan told him the tale.

"My girl," he said, turning to Jacqueline, "go away from here as speedily as thou canst. This man has the plague. It has broken out in several parts of the city, owing to bad food or none at all, and this man has caught it. Thou art exposing thyself to a terrible disease and almost certain death. This is no place for thee. Go home, and I will take care of the man to the best of my ability, but I doubt if he will live, even so."

Jacqueline's eyes opened wide with a startled look, and she glanced uncertainly at Jan. The sick man stirred restlessly, then with a sudden cry muttered her name in his feverish sleep. At that word, the girl formed her decision.

"I will not go, Dr. de Witt. This man has been a friend to me and mine ever since I can remember. I do not fear the plague, and even if I did, it would not keep me from giving all the aid I could to Jan Van Buskirk. Moreover, I know a little about medicine myself, having read it in an old book in my possession. I have raised healing herbs, and I also possess one which has the power, they say, to protect from such diseases if carried about the person. I will always have it by me, for I wish to help you in nursing this my friend back to life and health." Dr. de Witt looked her over for a moment in silent astonishment. Then he spoke:

"Thou art a brave maiden, whoever thou art, and I would that there were many more like thee! Help me thou shalt if such is thy determination, and the good God will bless thee and protect thee from all harm. There is much in having absolutely no fear of this contagion, and I see thou hast none. With thy help we may perhaps save our old friend and neighbor." Together they labored over the old man, and before he left, the doctor expressed his amazed approval of the skill and knowledge exhibited by this fair slip of a girl in tending and administering to the sick. Beyond this too, something in her manner, her look and her speech indefinably recalled to him old recollections.

"Thou dost constantly put me in mind of someone," he remarked finally. "Hadst thou ever any relation who was a physician? What is thy father?"

"I have no father," answered the girl with the reticence she had learned to exhibit through Vrouw Voorhaas's teaching. "He is long since dead."

"But what is thy last name?" persisted the good doctor.

"Coovenden," replied Jacqueline with the hesitancy she could never quite overcome in pronouncing this assumed title.

"Coovenden? Ah, it is not a name that I recognize—and yet there is something—I know not what, which stirs me!" And he went away shaking his head thoughtfully. On her way home Jacqueline stopped at the public market to purchase what scarce supply of provisions she was able to obtain.

"But this is a miserable little cabbage!" she expostulated mildly to the huckster who served her. "And see! This mutton-bone has scarce any meat upon it. 'Twill be watery soup that is made from this mess!"

"And lucky thou art to have any soup at all!" answered the

market woman. "I tell thee, girl, the time is coming when we shall be glad to eat the grass that grows in the streets, and that's not far distant either. I, for one, would gladly see the gates opened to the Spaniards. They are better at least than slow starvation!" Jacqueline shrank away from her at these words, so like disloyalty to the great cause, and hurried home with the news she had to tell.

As the day wore on, Vrouw Voorhaas became more and more uneasy about Gysbert and questioned his sister so closely about his absence that she had hard work quieting the woman's fears and at the same time hiding the truth about him. She herself was beset by more definite terrors for his safety than Vrouw Voorhaas could even guess and, though she did not expect Gysbert before nightfall, counted the moments with ever-increasing agitation.

Then darkness came and the two partook of their frugal supper, laying aside a generous portion for the boy. One by one the stars twinkled out. Jacqueline, sitting by the window, tried to count them to distract her thoughts. Her mind reverted again and again to the scenes of the morning, and the pictures of the suffering she had witnessed would not fade from her consciousness. As she sat leaning her head against the casement, she was suddenly startled by having two hands clapped over her eyes and a voice whispering in her ear:

"Guess who it is!"

"Gysbert!" she exclaimed. "How didst thou get in?"

"Hush! I slipped in through the garden and climbed to my window up the rose trellis. I did not want Vrouw Voorhaas to see my disguise and have washed it all off and changed my clothes. Where is she?"

"In her room," answered his sister, "and right anxious about thee, I can warrant! But tell me all about it, Gysbert!"

In hasty sentences the boy told her of his day's adventures. She listened with breathless interest and shuddered not a few times at the narrowness of his escapes. Then she recounted to him her own experiences and told of Jan Van Buskirk's illness and danger. When she had finished, they sat together in the darkness for a long time without speaking. Finally Jacqueline took her brother's hand in hers and said:

"Gysbert, thine own bravery and the dark scenes I have witnessed today have set me thinking, and tonight I have made my resolve. Since thou hast given thyself to the dangerous task of assisting our beloved city, I, too, can do no less than devote myself to the relief of some of its suffering. Tomorrow I shall seek Dr. de Witt and ask him to allow me to accompany him in his visits to the sick and starving. I can aid in nursing them, at least, since God has given me that power."

Gysbert returned his sister's clasp but continued in silence for some moments. Truth to tell, he was struggling with a lump that had risen in his throat and was glad that the darkness hid the tears that had gathered under his lashes. The experience of the last few days and weeks had helped to give him a poise beyond his years, but his admiration for his sister's quiet courage almost deprived him of words with which to express it. Presently, however, he got up and put his arms around her neck.

"Jacqueline," he said, trying to master the huskiness in his voice, "thou art very brave. I would rather go ten times into the heart of the Spanish army than once into a room with the plague. But thou art right. It is thy destined work since thou hast chosen it, and our father, were he here, would surely say, 'Well done!'"

Chapter VI

The Coming of the First Pigeon

The middle of August found the conditions in Leyden in no way improved but rather the worse, being just so many weeks nearer starvation. The poor had reached a point where they were indeed glad to get what nourishment they might from the grass that grew in the streets, and even the leaves from the trees that shaded the canals. Even the rich now suffered from the scantiness of provisions and were fain to draw in their belts tightly to lessen the gnawing of constant hunger.

Jacqueline and Gysbert had lost their fresh, rosy complexions and the roundness of their youthful curves and looked white and thin. Yet they still fared better than some. Gysbert had made seven trips through the Spanish lines, each time bearing away two carrier pigeons and bringing back when he could a little supply of fresh food in his bag. The six remaining birds they had decided to kill and eat, one a week, so that they might have at least a taste of fresh, untainted meat occasionally. It had cost Jacqueline many a pang to thus sacrifice her pets, but she could not see her dear ones suffer when it was in her power to give them food.

Gysbert's latest excursion outside the city walls had been successful and without any of the excitement that had attended his first trip. He had chosen an entirely different quarter through which to pass and had met with either a friendly reception or indifference from those he met and who freely purchased his herbs.

He was taken without question for a Glipper, as he had announced himself to be, and his presence soon became a familiar figure in their midst. Then too, these expeditions were of much shorter duration than his first, since instead of traveling all the way to Delft, he had only to leave his message and the pigeons at the farmhouse of Julius Van Schaick, a short distance from the city. He had thus far managed also to escape the vigilance of Vrouw Voorhaas, who now accepted without question the explanation of his executing errands for the burgomaster.

And what of Jacqueline? Plague now raged through all the poorer sections of the city—a dread disease brought on by improper nourishment or none at all. Dr. de Witt and Jacqueline went their daily rounds, cheering, comforting, and administering medicine and nourishment on every side. Never was a presence more welcome in a sickroom than that of the slim, fair girl whom many in their delirium took to be an angel. Never was a touch more deft, light, and soothing than hers.

By her tender care, Jan Van Buskirk had been nursed through the awful scourge. He was still as weak as a baby yet able to crawl about his room listlessly and inquire after the progress of the siege. His admiration for and devotion to the girl who had brought him safely through his peril was beyond all expression, and he did little else when she was near than follow her with his eyes in an ecstasy of dumb admiration.

Vrouw Voorhaas utterly disapproved of Jacqueline's mission to the sick and spared no pains to make her disapproval known. She was constantly in terror lest the girl herself should become infected, and she scolded, muttered, and sighed whenever Jacqueline prepared to go out. But the young girl's determination was too firm to be shaken by the older woman's expostulations, and her interest and devotion to the work had grown with her increasing responsibility. Dr. de Witt secretly marveled at her quiet firmness, skill, and unflinching courage. More and more did he rack his brains to elucidate the mystery of her strange resemblance to someone he had once known or seen, but without result.

"Jacqueline, come up to Hengist Hill with me," said Gysbert one hot, oppressive day about the twentieth of August. "Thou dost look white and tired and needest a little change of air, and besides, I want to talk to thee."

"Ah, Gysbert, the day is too hot, and I am very tired! Let us rest here in the house instead," replied the girl wearily.

"Nay, the air is fresh and cool on the hill, and I have yet another reason for the expedition. Come with me and thou wilt not regret it." Yielding to his wish, Jacqueline accompanied him through the blazing, sun-baked streets, striving for once not to see the misery that now lay open to the daylight all about them. But Gysbert was right—the hill was a decided improvement on the heated atmosphere of the town. The grove was cool and pleasant, and a refreshing breeze swept the summit. They sat down in the shadow of the old fortress and drew in great breaths of the life-giving salt air.

"Ah, it is good to be here!" exclaimed Gysbert. "Art thou not glad we came, Jacqueline? And now let me ask a question. Answer truly! What hast thou had to eat today?"

"Oh, I had plenty!" answered the girl evasively. "The weather is so hot that I cannot eat much."

"Now, look thou here!" he replied. "For breakfast this morning we had some watery gruel of our pigeon grain and a thin slice of malt-cake apiece. I saw thee eat the gruel, but the cake disappeared quickly in some mysterious way. Jacqueline, didst thou save it to take to Jan?"

"Well, yes, I suppose so," she faltered, cornered so cleverly that she could not deny it.

"Very well!" replied Gysbert with decision. "Then I will tell him the next time I go there that thou art starving thyself to feed him!"

"No, no, Gysbert!" she cried in genuine alarm. "Thou must not do that! It would grieve him unto death, for I have told him that we have plenty."

"Ah! Does that worry thee? Then if thou wilt do something to please *me*, I promise not to tell him."

"Yes, yes," said Jacqueline eagerly. "Anything, Gysbert, will I do if thou wilt only keep that secret!" The boy did not answer, but running to the wall of the fortress, lifted a good-sized stone and took from the hollow underneath something which he brought to his sister. It was the legs and body of a wild rabbit which had been prepared and cooked evidently before an open fire.

"Why, Gysbert!" exclaimed Jacqueline in astonishment. "Where didst thou get this?"

"I brought down the rabbit with a stone, here on the hill early this morning. Then I skinned him, dressed him, built a fire and roasted him before it, and hid him away in a cool place for our treat this afternoon. Thou must eat exactly half of it now, or I will tell Jan all about thy deception."

"But Vrouw Voorhaas!" said the girl doubtfully. "We ought to take some of it to her."

"Nay," he answered. "I have watched her, and I know what she does, also. She would thank us and put it aside, only to present it to us at another meal, saying she could not eat it herself. And what is more, she never would eat it, if we left it till it rotted away, so we might just as well finish it now."

Together they divided the doubtful dainty and devoured it as though it were the perfection of epicurean cookery; never did a meal taste sweeter to these half-famished children as they sat nibbling the last vestige of meat from the bones and feeling new life renewed within them.

"Now," said Gysbert when they had finished, "let me tell thee all about my last trip through the besieging lines yesterday and the messages I bore. Mynheer Van der Werf sent very discouraged word to our good Prince of Orange. The city, he said, was on the brink of starvation, the bread was gone, and the malt-cakes would hold out but four days more. Moreover, the people had fulfilled the promise made in the beginning of the siege—they had held out two months with food and one month without, and human strength could do no more.

"Mynheer Paul Buys, himself, was at the farmhouse and took

the message and the pigeons. He said the number of birds was now sufficient and I need bring no more unless these should all return before the siege was over. Then he sent by word of mouth this reply to the burgomaster. 'The Prince begs you to hold out a few days more, as his scheme for relief has already begun to be put into execution. In a day or two a carrier pigeon will come from him telling all about it.'

"Jacqueline, I have guessed what that relief is going to be! A few chance words dropped by Mynheer Buys and an exclamation from the burgomaster has made me certain of it. Ah! It is a great thought—great indeed!—and like our wonderful Prince to dare it. Canst thou imagine what it is?"

"Nay," said the girl wonderingly, "I cannot."

"Look!" cried Gysbert, pointing in the direction of the ocean. "Dost thou see that huge bulk across the Rhine about five miles from here? That is the greatest outer barrier, the Land-scheiding. See how it keeps back the ocean? Dost thou guess now what is happening?"

"Not—" hesitated the girl, "not that the dykes have been pierced!"

"Just that! Just that!" cried her brother. "Is it not wonderful? The Prince is calling the ocean to his aid, since he cannot raise an army. The Spaniards will drown like rats in a tank!" Jacqueline looked doubtful and not quite convinced.

"But the land!" she said. "It will ruin all the farms and crops between here and the ocean. And think of all the labor that has been spent on the dykes to shut out the sea. When will they ever be able to rebuild these barriers and shut out the waters?"

"That will all come in good time," he replied. "First, it is most important to get rid of this Spanish pest. Did I not hear Mynheer Van der Werf himself mutter, 'Better a drowned land than a lost one!' It was this exclamation that put me on the track."

"Dost say that the Prince sends word that the scheme is already begun?" asked Jacqueline.

"Yes, and I think I know what he has done. Mynheer Buys was telling me that he has but lately been to Kappelle and Schiedam. I will wager that they have pierced the dykes all the way from here to Rotterdam, and even as far as Kappelle. But the tide does not rise high at this time of the year and there is only an east wind, so that the water flows in slowly. But see! See!" And he pointed far off in the sky, where a tiny speck floated—a mere golden moat in the sunshine. "I feel certain that is one of our pigeons, Jacqueline. He flies like 'William of Orange.'"

"Thou hast good eyes, Gysbert! I can see nothing but a faint speck. Let us watch it, though." Together they waited in breathless suspense while the speck drew nearer and assumed more definite shape.

"Look how the left wing droops a trifle. I *know* that is 'William of Orange!'" cried Gysbert. In an incredibly short time, the bird had passed the limits of the city wall, had drawn closer and closer, and at last passed directly over their heads.

So close to the summit of the hill was its flight that they could faintly hear the whir of its wings. When it was close above them, all doubt as to its identity vanished, and besides, it was making straight in the direction of Belfry Lane. Without waiting a moment, they rushed down the hill, their bodies refreshed by their meal of none too well-cooked rabbit meat, their courage restored by the hope of speedy deliverance for the city.

They found when they reached the house that the pigeon had been long before them, Vrouw Voorhaas declaring that she had let it in some half an hour previously. Up to the dovecote they clambered, breathless and excited, to behold "William of Orange" strutting about proudly, preening his ruffled feathers and cooing plaintively to be fed. Gysbert found a message tied about the bird's leg. As fast as his feet would carry him, he flew to the statehouse to deliver the precious bit of paper into the hands of Adrian Van der Werf. But Jacqueline, with a handful of corn, coaxed the weary messenger to alight on her arm. When he had eaten his fill, she cuddled his head under her soft chin and stroked his brilliant plumage.

"'William of Orange,'" she crooned, "thou art well-called. The city owes much to thee and to thy great namesake!"

Chapter VII

A Swim in the Canal and What Came of It

The message brought by the pigeon proved to be word direct from the Prince of Orange himself to the people of Leyden. He implored them to take courage and explained what means he had taken to effect their relief. The plan was what Gysbert had suspected but was of even wider scope. Not only had all the dykes been ruptured and the water had begun to rise upon the Landscheiding, but also the Prince had been rapidly collecting provisions in all the principal cities and towns nearby and was loading them on a fleet of vessels ready to sail across the land to Leyden when the flood would permit. Thus the same waters that were to rout the Spanish army were to bear life and food to the suffering city. It was truly a daring and original plan, and Van der Werf's stern, harassed countenance lighted with joy when he read the missive.

"Ring the bells!" he commanded. "Call a meeting of the populace in the great square! Order the military bands to play inspiriting music! Fire the cannons and sing lustily! Surely this news must put heart into the people!"

Then such a bedlam of sounds as rose within the walls of Leyden! Not for months had there been such a stir and life in the streets of the half-dead city. The Spaniards outside, hearing the revelry and not in the least understanding its cause, gazed at each other in amazement and could only conjecture that a great army must be coming to the relief of their foes. But they were not long to remain in doubt. That night a sentinel rushed into the camp shouting:

"The water! The water! It stands ten inches deep all round the outskirts of the Land-scheiding! The dykes have all been pierced!" And swift consternation seized them as they began to grasp the meaning of the shouts of joy within the walls of Leyden.

But a week passed, and the waters did not continue to rise. The low tides and the constant east winds were most unfavorable to the present flooding of the land. Confidence was restored to the Spanish army, and in the city the recent joy faded away as suddenly as it had come. Dull distrust reigned unchecked, and the Glippers, of whom there were not a few in the town, lost no opportunity to scoff at "this mad, hopeless scheme of the Prince's," as they called it.

"Go up to the tower on Hengist Hill," they would cry scornfully to the patriots, "and *see* if the ocean is coming over the dry land to your relief!" Then it came to be that Hengist Hill was haunted day and night by anxious, hunger-stricken men and women, watching, hoping, trusting, praying that some help might come to the famished city.

Meantime, the weather continued stifling and unbearable, and sickness, death, and the plague raged in Leyden. Jacqueline had her heart and hands full with her newly assumed duties. But Gysbert, not having lately any mission to execute beyond the walls, found time hanging rather heavily on his hands. One muggy, oppressive morning he determined, for lack of anything better to do, to seek some secluded spot and indulge in a refreshing swim in one of the less-frequented canals.

Reaching a shaded spot sufficiently isolated for his purpose, he divested himself of his garments, plunged in, and remained for half an hour swimming about idly in the cool water. At length concluding that his bath had been long enough, he drew himself out and was about to resume his clothes when he happened to glance down the road that led by the canal. About a hundred yards ahead, a black-cloaked figure whose rear view struck him as somewhat familiar was hurrying stealthily along.

"By St. Pancras!" muttered Gysbert. "If that isn't Dirk Willumhoog again! There's mischief afoot!" Dropping his clothes, he ran down the bank, slipped without noise into the water, and swam hurriedly in the direction of the retreating figure.

"If I keep behind him close and to the bank," thought the boy, "I can watch him very well, and he'll never suspect there is a soul around." It did not take him long to catch up with the man he was pursuing. Most of the time he kept out of sight, but he rose occasionally far enough to poke his head over the edge of the canal and peep at his enemy. Once as he did so, he dropped back quickly, finding that Dirk had seated himself under a tree not five feet away. The man was busily engaged in examining the writing on some scraps of paper, or he would certainly have seen the wet, tousled head poked suddenly up over the bank.

"Whew!" thought Gysbert as he ducked, "but that was a narrow escape! I wonder how long he's going to sit mooning there! 'Tis right unpleasant hanging here motionless, and in spite of the heat, the water grows chilly." But Dirk had evidently no intention of moving at present, and Gysbert was obliged to shiver and wait for some time before the spirit moved the man to be gone. At length the crunch of footsteps on the gravel warned the boy that his enemy was once more on his way. It was a relief to swim again and limber up his stiffened body, but to his astonishment he found that they were drawing near to an unfrequented portion of the city near the walls and that the canal-street would soon turn off in another direction.

"Where *can* he be going?" questioned Gysbert as he poked up his head at the turn and saw Dirk advancing straight on, apparently right to the wall itself. At that moment the man half turned his head, and Gysbert ducked under hastily. When he again raised himself, to his amazement, Dirk had disappeared as completely as though the earth had opened up and swallowed him.

"Has the rascal spread his cloak and *flown* over the wall, or has he changed his bodily substance and passed right through it, like the prince in the fairy tale?" demanded Gysbert of the air about him. But as it was plain this would bring no solution of the enigma, he cautiously crept toward the wall, determined by some means to solve the mystery.

From the turn of the canal to the wall was a distance of perhaps five hundred yards, an unoccupied space of ground like a meadow, broken by nothing save a little brook that connected with the canal. At the base of the wall, this brook spread out for a space, like a miniature lake. Gysbert examined every inch of the ground attentively without finding anything that might serve to enlighten him. At the face of the wall he stopped. Plainly, no human being could scale at this point the high, smooth surface that confronted him. Dropping on his knees, he examined the base. "Nothing here!" he muttered, and waded into the tiny lake that spread out before him.

Step by step he advanced, feeling carefully of the brick wall at every interval to detect any possible weak spot, when suddenly his feet slipped into a deep hole. He was drawn under and swept by the force of some swift current through a small, hidden aperture in the wall. When he came to the surface, he grasped at a projecting ledge and tried to ascertain what had happened. It did not take him long to guess. The marshy land in and about Leyden was constantly intersected by the formation of new brooks and streams. Not infrequently they would undermine the very wall itself, and in times of peace, these defects were always carefully watched and remedied. But in the terrible strain under which the city had existed for the past months, this one had evidently passed unnoticed, and in truth, no one would have suspected its presence from the inside of the city, so well was it hidden by the little spreading lake.

"Now what ought I do next?" thought Gysbert when he had unraveled this mystery. "Without doubt this is Dirk's secret doorway, and how he discovered it the Evil One only knows! The question is, should I try to explore it before he is well out of the way? I would hardly care to meet him in this black hole! On the other hand, I don't believe he will remain in here a moment longer than he has to, and I'm freezing hanging here. I'll risk it!"

So saying, he plunged into the grim cave and commenced his journey through the base of the great wall of Leyden. To his disgust, he found that the stream did not penetrate straight from side to side, but turned and pierced through the *length* of the wall for many yards. The way was difficult enough, since he had to fight every inch of his progress against the swift current, and once the water deepened to such an extent that he was forced to swim. Moreover, unwarmed by any sun, it was icy cold, and his limbs grew numb and his teeth chattered.

For a moment panic seized him, and he felt sure he would never get out alive, but would drown in this horrible place. Then his natural courage again asserted itself, and he pressed steadily forward. At length the course of the hidden stream changed again, a faint glimmer of daylight appeared, and in another moment he stood outside the walls of Leyden, protected from the gaze of the Spanish camp only by a few bushes. No Dirk Willumhoog was to be seen, but there remained not a shadow of doubt that this was his mode of ingress to and exit from the city of Leyden.

Gysbert lay down in the sunlight and warmed his numbed body in its welcome heat. In half an hour's time he had started on his return trip and found it twice as easy as traveling in the opposite direction. Far from fighting the current, he was helped along by it and in a short time stood safe within the town again. Arrived there, another swim awaited him, for as he could not run through the town clad in nothing at all, he was obliged to take to the canal till he reached the spot where he had left his clothes. Once only he stopped to climb out and investigate the place where Dirk had sat examining his papers. As good luck would have it, he discovered hidden away in the grass, where it had evidently fallen unnoticed, one of the scraps. On it were written a few words, evidently only a part of the whole, whatever that might have been. Gysbert read them, and his eyes grew big with wonder and then snapped angrily. "Ah, this is shameful!" he cried. "We'll see about this, Dirk Willumhoog, thou traitor as well as coward!"

With the paper in his mouth for safety, he plunged into the canal, swam to the point where he had left his clothes, flung them on hastily, and hurried home as fast as he could run.

"I shall have something to tell Jacqueline about *this* day's work!" he remarked to himself with great satisfaction.

Chapter VIII

"Tranquil amid Raging Billows"

Jacqueline was not at home when Gysbert arrived hot and breathless. She had been out all morning with Dr. de Witt on their usual errand of mercy, and Vrouw Voorhaas declared with much sullen complaining that she could not be expected for an hour yet. So the boy was compelled to fret and wander about idly till she appeared. When she came, she looked desperately tired, but she ascended cheerfully to the dovecote with her brother, which place he chose as the safest and most secluded in which to impart his secret.

"I had the greatest adventure this morning, Jacqueline!" he began. And while she listened eagerly, petting the smooth head of her finest pigeon and coaxing him with a little grain, Gysbert told of his swim in the canal and its results. When he came to the part concerning the discovery of the paper, he pulled it from his pocket and showed it to her. It was, as has been said, only a portion of the whole writing and commenced at the top with the completion of some sentence begun on another piece:

> "—evidently in Belfry Lane.
> The Prince is dangerously ill
> in Rotterdam. We have conveyed
> to him the report that Leyden
> has surrendered. While this is
> not yet true, the news will so

discourage him that it is doubtful if he will recover—"

"Canst thou imagine anything more despicable than that?" exclaimed Gysbert. "Our good Prince sickened unto death by such reports! Something must be done about it."

"Shall thou go at once and tell Mynheer Van der Werf?" inquired his sister.

"Well, I suppose I should, but then he would only send me off at once to deny the rumor, so I may just as well not lose the time."

"But, Gysbert, what can that mean at the first?" said Jacqueline, "'—evidently in Belfry Lane.' Can it possibly refer to us?"

"I do not doubt that it is just what it does refer to," he replied. "He has, most likely, found out where we live. He means mischief, I tell thee, not only to the country but to us also, though what we have done to merit his attention, I cannot imagine."

"Thou didst anger him, Gysbert, that day at the gate, and he has not forgotten. But there is something else beside. What can it be? Ah, I fear harm is coming to us!"

"Well, I for one am not going to think about that, when this other matter is so much more important," replied Gysbert characteristically. "This very night I shall disguise myself as usual and make one more trip through the camp. As I must travel all the way to Rotterdam, I may not return for two or three days, so thou must explain it as best thou canst to Vrouw Voorhaas. I do not care much now what thou dost tell her, for she can do little to prevent my getting away if I choose."

"Ah, brother, I dread to have thee go! These be evil times, and I have a foreboding that all will not go well whilst thou art away. And yet I would not keep thee, for 'tis more than wicked that our Prince should be so ill and so cruelly deceived. But thou must take a pigeon with thee and send him to me with a message if thou art detained over long, else I shall break my heart with anxiety watching for thee."

At dawn next morning Gysbert set forth in his usual disguise carrying the pigeon "William of Orange" at the bottom of his bag of herbs. Passing out through the gate of the Tower of Burgundy, he chose a route through a part of the army near that of his first attempt, since that way lay nearer to the road for Delft and Rotterdam. The usual sleeping camp lay all about him. The usual challenge from drowsy sentinels arrested his progress, but thanks to the magic countersign, "*Don Carlos*," which he had learned from the gatekeeper, he was nowhere detained. He accomplished the passage of the camp with absolutely no molestation or exciting incident, thinking that the feat was becoming very, very easy.

On the road to Delft he looked along the canal to see if he might spy Joris Fruytiers and his bulky craft. But the canal was deserted, and he was obliged to make up his mind that his own two feet must carry him most of the way. As he trudged along, he could not but notice the exceeding muddiness of the road, and the farther he proceeded, the worse did it become, till at length he found himself plowing through a veritable bog.

"This is singular!" was his first thought, and then, "Why, no it isn't either! This is the result of the broken-down dykes. How strange that I did not think of it at first!" And the worse it became, the more it pleased him, since it might mean ultimate relief and victory to the city. Finally he found himself wading through several inches of water, and he took infinite, boyish delight in slopping through its muddy depths, splashing the drops from side to side as he walked. In due time he reached Delft and stopped to get a hearty meal at a baker's shop with a few coins he had in his pocket. Thus refreshed and rested, he continued on his way.

Darkness at length overtook him, and abandoning all hope of reaching Rotterdam that night, he crept into a farmer's barn and in the hayloft slept the sleep of healthy weariness till the first streaks of dawn tinted the horizon. Trudging on his road again, without either a breakfast or the prospect of one, it was noon before he reached the goal of his desire, Rotterdam, where lay ill and despairing the idol of his boyish dreams, William, Prince of Orange-Nassau.

Gysbert had never been in Rotterdam; consequently, he was compelled to inquire his way frequently. Ascertaining that the Prince was then stopping at a house on the Hoog Straat, and being directed to that thoroughfare, he was not long in arriving at his destination. It was a much smaller establishment than the palace of the *Prinsenhof* in Delft, and to the boy's astonishment, there seemed to be absolutely no one about the premises. The large front entrance was not locked, and having knocked in vain for many minutes, he pushed open the door and entered.

Nothing greeted him but deserted halls and rooms. He lingered about in the corridors for a while, hoping that someone might come in. Then his attention became attracted by occasional groans and muttered ejaculations from the room above. Fearing that someone, possibly the Prince himself, might be in trouble, he decided to go up and see if he might render any assistance. He crept up softly and, guided by the sounds, reached an open doorway and peeped in.

Tossing and moaning on a bed lay the gaunt form of a man. One glance sufficed to convince Gysbert that it was William of Orange and that he was desperately ill. Why the great head of his country should be thus deserted by every one of his attendants in his trouble was more than Gysbert could fathom. A natural hesitancy, however, kept him from intruding on the privacy of the sick man's bedroom, and he stood outside for a time, watching and wondering if there were anything he might do.

The Prince lay in a huge, four-post bed raised on a sort of dias or platform. At his feet on the coverlet sat a little brown-and-white spaniel, who whined plaintively as if in answer to his master's groans. When Gysbert appeared in the doorway, the animal sprang up, barking furiously, and tried to wake his master. But the Prince was at the time in a sort of stupor and paid no heed to the animal's cries. The dog soon perceived that the intruder attempted no harm and settled himself in his former post.

Gysbert knew well why the Prince was attended by this faithful beast. Two years before at the siege of Mons, he had been surprised one night while asleep in his tent by a party of Spaniards who had planned to capture him. A little spaniel who slept in his quarters sprang up, barking and scratching his hands. The Prince, thus wakened, found time to escape, but had it not been for the faithful little animal, the Netherlands would have lost their strongest protector. For the rest of his life, the Prince was never without a spaniel of the same breed who slept nightly in his room.

Gysbert had ample time to note what manner of man was this his idol. His forehead was high, noble, and marked with many lines of care. The expression of his face, even racked with burning fever, was of a tender, strong, and fatherly benignity. Nearby lay his armor and sword, on the hilt of which was carved in Latin his chosen motto:

"*Saevis tranquillus in undis!*"

("Tranquil amid raging billows!")

No language could have better expressed the quiet firmness and unshaken courage of this wonderful nobleman, even in the most harrowing and adverse circumstances.

The sick man was gradually emerging from unconsciousness. His eyes opened widely but unseeingly, and he muttered in a half-delirium:

"Ah, Leyden, Leyden! I pray that I might help thee! It is not true, it cannot be true that thou hast yielded to the enemy! Ah, my country! What fate is now before thee, and I so helpless to render thee aid!—Tranquil, tranquil!—I must be tranquil amid the billows!—Oh, thou my God, help me!—" Again unconsciousness overcame him, and he sank into another stupor. Gysbert's heart ached with pity and the wild desire to tell him that his fears were groundless. "When he next wakes," thought the boy, "I will go in and tell him how false is this report he has heard." Presently, the Prince exhibited signs of returning consciousness, but he seemed weaker and could only murmur:

"Leyden!—Leyden!—Tranquil—" Then Gysbert, with trembling knees and quaking heart, entered the door and walked up to the bed. At first the Prince did not see him, but soon the renewed barking of his spaniel attracted his attention to the curious little figure standing by the bedside.

"Who art thou?" he queried feebly.

"Mynheer Prince," faltered Gysbert, "I am only a boy from Leyden, but I have come to tell you that it is not true—what you have been told concerning the city's surrender. Leyden still holds out and will so continue till its last defender is slain!" The dullness of fever in the sick man's eyes gave place to an actual sparkle.

"Leyden still safe!" he exclaimed. "Then have I surely been deceived. Oh, God be praised that He has answered my prayer! But tell me, brave little fellow, how camest thou to know what only one of my confidential servants has whispered to me, and how camest thou all this way to undeceive me? Methinks too, thou hast assumed something of a disguise." Then Gysbert told him the circumstances of the finding of the paper, and much about Dirk Willumhoog. From this the Prince beguiled him into telling about how he had made expeditions with messages through the Spanish army and how his sister was helping care for the sick and plague-stricken in Leyden, and many details about the condition of the city. When he had finished, he was emboldened to ask the Prince how it was that the house had no attendants, especially when he lay so ill.

"Truly it must seem strange!" answered William the Silent. "I have the kindest of servants, and the best medical attendance, but it so happens that I have sent all off this morning on errands of the greatest importance. When this traitor, this Joachim Hansleer, returns, I will discharge him straightway for a lying villain who thinks to kill me by his deception. He has been whispering to me this past week that Leyden had surrendered but that the rest were afraid to tell me!"

"If the great Prince would forgive me for saying it," replied Gysbert, "I would suggest that he be locked up in close confinement instead, else he will join his companion, Dirk Willumhoog, and plot more wickedness!"

"True, true!" exclaimed the Prince, laughing for the first time in weeks. "Thou art a clever lad to have thought of it. And now tell me thy name. I shall not forget thee." When Gysbert had told him, he held out his hand:

"Take these ten florins and buy thyself all the food thou canst carry back with thee. Be sure to tell Van der Werf to guard that opening in the wall well and arrest Dirk Willumhoog if he enters again. Tell him also that help is very near, and pray God for a west wind. My grateful thanks go with thee! Already I feel the fever abated, and new life surging through me. Farewell!" Gysbert knelt to kiss the hand of his hero and then sped away light of heel and glad of heart at the successful outcome of his errand.

And when, a few moments later, the Receiver-General of Holland, Cornelius Van Meirop, ascended to the bedchamber to visit his Prince, he marveled at the great change for the better that had suddenly taken place in the condition of William the Silent.

Chapter IX

Vrouw Voorhaas's Secret

No sooner had Gysbert been dispatched on his journey to Rotterdam than Jacqueline turned her attention to preparing breakfast. Much to her astonishment, Vrouw Voorhaas was not yet up and about, but she concluded that the woman was wearied out with hard work and anxiety and was taking an extra, involuntary nap.

The most careful search in the larder revealed nothing that under ordinary circumstances would be considered in the least palatable. Jacqueline remembered two pigeons' eggs that had been laid the day before and determined that they must go toward furnishing the breakfast table. These, with some very thin gruel of pigeon grain, completed the arrangements. Wondering that Vrouw Voorhaas had not yet appeared, and fearing lest something were the matter, she decided to go up and investigate the cause of this unusual state of affairs. At the door of the bedroom she paused, horror-struck at the sound of a curious muttering and groaning now grown terribly familiar to her ears. Then she opened the door. Her worst suspicions were verified—Vrouw Voorhaas had the plague!

The woman lay tossing and moaning, utterly unconscious of anything about her, muttering strange, incoherent sentences in her delirium. Amazed and shocked at what she heard, Jacqueline stood rooted to the spot, listening.

"I will not eat it!—I must not eat it!—" cried the unconscious woman. "—It is for the children!—Oh, how I hunger!—" Then in a lower tone: "Dirk Willumhoog, thou shalt *not* harm them as thou didst endeavor to harm—" Here she appeared to fall into a restless sleep, and for a few moments her tossing form lay quiet; Jacqueline buried her face in her hands and wept with sheer bitterness and despair.

"Oh, Vrouw Voorhaas, Vrouw Voorhaas!—Now I know what doth ail thee!" she sobbed aloud. "Thou hast starved thyself for our sakes; thou didst deceive us into thinking thou wast satisfied with a little, and now thou art reaping the results of thy sacrifice!" The realization that this faithful servant had brought herself to this pass by her own self-denial occupied Jacqueline's mind to the exclusion of every other thought. "How wicked and ungrateful I have been," she blamed herself, "going out to nurse other people when starvation and illness lay waiting right at my own door, and I never guessed! Oh, if Gysbert were only here!"

Then the necessity for doing something, and that speedily, forced itself upon her. Deciding that she could leave the sick woman more easily now than later, she ran out at once to find Dr. de Witt. He accompanied her without an instant's delay. When he reached the sickroom, he gave one keen glance at his patient and then set about his work of relief, Jacqueline assisting him with the intelligence and skill perfected by much practice.

"Now," said he finally, "thou must make up thy mind, Juffrouw Jacqueline, to one thing. For the present, thou must give up all thought of going on thy daily round with me and devote thyself to the care of this thy companion. Her case is more critical than usual, having been brought on, I judge, by systematic starvation."

"But Jan!—" faltered the girl. "He is still very weak and needs my care."

"Let him come here and stay," ordered the doctor. "I will myself fetch him this afternoon, and thus thou wilt have both thy patients under thine eye. He also may be able to help thee a little. Where is thy brother?"

"He has gone out of the city on an errand of importance. I do not expect him back for two or three days," she answered.

"Well, keep him out of the sickroom when he returns. 'Tis best for him not to be exposed to the disease. Now I must be going on my usual way. I shall miss thy helpful presence much, Juffrouw Jacqueline. Ah, but times are sore in this wretched city!" As he turned to go, Vrouw Voorhaas roused herself and began muttering anew:

"Louvain?—Louvain?—Yes, from there we came, but what is that to thee!—" The doctor started and walked back toward his patient.

"She hath been raving much without sense!" remarked Jacqueline hastily. "I fear her mind is all unhinged!" But Dr. de Witt continued to scrutinize sharply the features of the sick woman.

"Didst thou really come from Louvain?" he asked Jacqueline at length.

"Yes," faltered the girl, "many years ago."

"What is the name of this woman?" the doctor continued to question. As Jacqueline told him, a great light appeared to break in on his mind.

"Ah, ah!" he exclaimed. "I see it all! It is as clear as day to me now! That resemblance in thee I was sure I should place sometime. Is not thy name Cornellisen, and was not thy father the famous doctor-professor in the University?"

"Aye!" answered Jacqueline in fear and trembling. "Thou hast guessed aright, but tell no one, I pray thee!"

"I knew it! I felt it!" continued the doctor. "And yet I could not make the memory a connected one, till now. I was a student about to graduate from the University, and thy father was my great admiration and example. I saw Vrouw Voorhaas once on visiting his home but never his children, hence I did not recognize thee. It was sad—sad, thy father's end, and I grieved over it many a long day! It was his great devotion to the young Count de Buren, who was under his special care, that brought him to his death. Dost thou know all about it?"

"I know only what Vrouw Voorhaas has told me, of his being captured and killed by the cruel Duke of Alva," answered Jacqueline.

"Then I can tell thee more, and I will sometime. Right glad I am that it has fallen to my lot to help and befriend thee, for so I can render service to thy dead father who was always more than kind to me."

All the morning Jacqueline sat by the sick woman's bedside, moistening her parched lips with water, cooling her feverish brow with refreshing compresses, and tending to every unspoken want with a devotion born of love and remorse. At no time did Vrouw Voorhaas become sane and conscious of her surroundings, and her feverish delirium increased as the day wore on. It wrung the girl's tender heart to hear her cry out against the pangs of hunger and imagine that she must continually deny herself for the children's sake.

Little by little, the history of all the past weeks of suffering was revealed to the watching girl, and she realized that what she had supposed to be a sufficient supply of provisions for all had only been rendered enough for herself and Gysbert by the cruel deprivation of this faithful woman. But other chance ejaculations were more mystifying and served to arouse in Jacqueline an intense, terrified curiosity as to what might be this long-kept secret that so troubled the soul of Vrouw Voorhaas. Once she was electrified by hearing the sick woman hiss:

"How didst thou get in the city, Dirk Willumhoog?—No, go away! Thou canst draw nothing from me!—I will not tell thee, I say!—Thou dare not touch one hair of their heads!—Nay, I will not tell thee!—Keep thy gold!—What do I care for all the wealth of the Indies?—Their father—"

Jacqueline puzzled over it in trembling astonishment. Was it possible that Dirk Willumhoog had been here in Belfry Lane and interviewed Vrouw Voorhaas while they were away somewhere? But why had she not told them of it? What could be this dreadful mystery that the two seemed to share in common? What harm did he plan to do them?

That afternoon Jan arrived, accompanied by Dr. de Witt. Jacqueline now had her hands full with the two patients, but she was grateful for the companionship of the old man. It had seemed unutterably depressing to be shut up alone with this sick woman who was never for a moment in her right mind and who raved incessantly about disturbing mysteries. Two more days passed, and the conditions in Belfry Lane continued about the same. Vrouw Voorhaas did not improve, except that she had less delirium, and Jacqueline was worried almost out of her senses because Gysbert had not yet appeared. Nothing could convince her that all was well with him, and she kept constant watch for the carrier pigeon to bring some news.

Running up to the cote on the fourth day, she found, to her joy, "William of Orange" strutting about among the two or three other birds. A note was fastened about his leg, and Jacqueline unfastened it with trembling, eager fingers. To her surprise it was addressed not to her but to Vrouw Voorhaas and was in a strange handwriting. With a great throb of terror, she opened it and read these words:

"Vrouw Voorhaas,
Fortune has at last turned in my favor. The boy is now in my possession, and before long the girl will be also. I snap my fingers in thy face!
Dirk Willumhoog."

Chapter X

The Beggars of the Sea

"Vrouw Voorhaas is decidedly better today, Juffrouw Jacqueline," remarked Dr. Pieter de Witt as he left the bedside of the sick woman. "She is really coming out of this illness very well, thanks to thy careful nursing and our good Jan's assistance."

"Is it so indeed?" answered Jacqueline listlessly, striving to force herself to some show of enthusiasm. "Then am I right glad, for I have done my best, and thou hast been devotion itself, Dr. de Witt. Oh! If only—" She turned away her head to hide the tears that would come, and a sob stopped her further utterance. The good doctor understood and busied himself over his patient till the girl had regained her self-control.

"If I mistake not," he ventured at length, "she will probably be quite herself today, having regained consciousness several times lately. It would be well, should she recover sufficiently to ask after thy brother, not to allow her to think he has come to harm. A shock like that would thrust her lower than she has yet been."

"But what shall we say?" faltered Jacqueline. "I must not tell an untruth."

"Wouldst thou tell her the broad, brutal facts, and thereby cause her death?" demanded the doctor sternly. "Nay, it is only necessary to say that since she had been suffering with the plague, it was deemed wisest to send him away for a time, lest he contract the disease. She will be satisfied with that for the present." Jacqueline acquiesced in this, and the two went downstairs to acquaint Jan Van Buskirk with the news of the improvement in Vrouw Voorhaas's condition. Jan was sitting in the sunny, immaculate kitchen reading his big Bible, one of the few possessions he had brought with him to Belfry Lane. He was as pleased as the others with the good report.

"Listen to this!" he remarked. "I've just been reading it in the Good Book. I think the Lord must have had the siege of Leyden in mind when He caused this to be written—'Surely He shall deliver thee from the snare of the fowler and from the noisome pestilence!'—Isn't that just what happened to Vrouw Voorhaas and myself! I call it nothing less than miraculous! And here's some more!—'Thou shalt not be afraid for the terror by night, nor for the arrow that flieth by day'—Doesn't that just describe the Spanish army out beyond!—'Nor for the pestilence that walketh in darkness'—that's the plague—'Nor for the destruction that wasteth at noonday.'—That's starvation!

"'A thousand shall fall at thy side, and ten thousand at thy right hand, but it shall not come nigh thee!' Haven't more than five thousand died of starvation and the pestilence here already, and we are yet spared!"

"True, true!" murmured Jacqueline. "But Gysbert!—" Now there was an unspoken but well-understood conspiracy between the doctor and Jan to keep up the spirits of the despairing girl on this painful subject.

"Thou didst not let me read far enough, Jacqueline," the old man hastened to add. "Only listen! Here is another Psalm that I was reading this morning. It should be a great help to thee: 'The Lord is my light and my salvation; whom shall I fear? The Lord is the strength of my life; of whom shall I be afraid?

"'When the wicked, even mine enemies, came upon me to eat up my flesh, they stumbled and fell. Though an host should encamp against me, my heart shall not fear. Though war should rise against me, in this will I be confident.

"'Teach me thy way, O Lord, and lead me in a plain path because of mine enemies. Wait on the Lord; be of good courage and He shall strengthen thine heart. Wait, I say, on the Lord!'"

"What thou hast read does truly give me new courage," said Jacqueline. "Thanks, Jan! Thou art indeed a help and a comfort. And now I will go up to the dovecote to see if perchance a pigeon has come with some message for the burgomaster."

A week had passed since the disappearance of the boy, and not a sign or a token had come to the anxious watchers in Belfry Lane to indicate his whereabouts or his fate. After the first shock caused by Dirk's message, Jacqueline had gone straight to Adrian Van der Werf and explained the situation, imploring him to assist in trying to find and rescue her brother. The burgomaster was deeply distressed at the misfortune that had come to his little jumper and was much mystified as to the cause of this continued persecution of two innocent children by an unknown man.

But as to offering any assistance, that, he told Jacqueline, was quite beyond his power. Already, concern for the famishing, besieged city and despair at its vanishing hopes of relief had driven him almost beyond his senses with anxiety. It was now not only impossible, but would be also quite fruitless for him to send men outside the walls to search for Gysbert, as they would probably be killed on sight by the ferocious Spaniards. He advised Jacqueline to wait quietly for further developments and gave it as his opinion that Gysbert had not been killed but was probably being kept alive for some yet unknown purpose. But little encouraged by this interview, Jacqueline crept home to endure silent but unending misery. For she was too proud to be seen by the others constantly grieving, and moreover, she blamed herself bitterly for ever allowing her brother to undertake such a hazardous enterprise.

Ascending to the pigeon-loft that morning, she found a returned messenger strutting about among the remaining birds. He bore a note wrapped round his leg, addressed to Adrian Van der Werf. Jacqueline made all haste to carry this to the statehouse, for it now devolved upon her to be the bearer of these messages when they arrived. The burgomaster welcomed her kindly:

"Good morning, Juffrouw Jacqueline! Hast heard any news from thy brother yet?"

"Nay," answered the girl, shaking her head sadly. "But I have here another message for you, Mynheer Van der Werf. It has but just come by a pigeon."

"Thanks, thanks!" he said, opening it eagerly. Then, with sparkling eyes, he cried:

"Ah, this is excellent, excellent news! Admiral Boisot, with his fleet manned by the Beggars of the Sea, has arrived out of Zeeland and is already entering the Rhine over the broken dykes. He cannot be ten miles from the city! Praise God, praise God!" He turned to Jacqueline for an answering enthusiasm but found to his surprise that the poor girl had fainted away in the chair where she sat, evidently from sheer hunger and fatigue. Van der Werf hastened to a closet, took out a bottle, and forced some cordial between her set teeth. As he chafed her cold hands he murmured:

"Poor, poor little girl! Thou hast borne thy share of this cursed trouble nobly and well—that I know from De Witt himself. Thou shalt have every comfort and help that I can render thee!" Jacqueline soon returned to consciousness, but the burgomaster would not yet allow her to leave and insisted that she drink another glass of the revivifying cordial. When she was quite herself again, he sent her back to Belfry Lane with a large basket of food from his own larder, which he had dispatched a soldier to procure.

"It is not much," he apologized, "for we are hard put to it ourselves for sustenance now. But it is at least something I can do for so faithful a helper. See that thou dost not stint *thyself* in thy distribution of it!" he ended laughing.

When she had gone, Van der Werf hastened to dispatch a town crier to spread the good news and himself made all speed to Hengist Hill to observe the position of the fleet. The day was clear, and the flotilla lay in plain sight, not far beyond the Land-scheiding—a motley array of more than two hundred vessels of every conceivable shape and size. The largest, an enormous craft with shot-proof bulwarks and moved by huge paddle wheels turned by a crank, was called the *Ark of Delft*. It served as the flagship for Admiral Boisot and was renowned for being the leader in every battle. Each ship carried from eight to ten cannon, and the whole fleet was manned by twenty-five hundred wild and battle-scarred veterans, the bravest and fiercest in the land.

They called themselves the "Beggars of the Sea," a name they had assumed since a time at first, when the scornful Spanish soldiery had mocked them. "Who is afraid of you! You are nothing but a pack of *beggars!*" scoffed the Spaniards. "Very well!" replied the hot-headed Zeelanders. "Ye shall see how *beggars* can *fight!*" And truly they made a ferocious crew, as the Spanish found later to their surprise and dismay. They neither gave nor took quarter, for theirs was a battle to the death, and woe to the luckless Spaniard who fell within their power! "Long live the Beggars!" was their rallying cry, and "Long live the Beggars!" now echoed in shout upon shout from Hengist Hill by the crowds that had followed the burgomaster to the summit. Hope was once more restored, and Leyden gathered herself together and drew a long breath of renewed courage.

But before the consummation of this hope, there was much to be done and many battles to fight. The Land-scheiding lay before the fleet guarded by Spanish troops, and all about, the villages and fortresses were in the hands of the same enemy. On the night of September 10, the city was startled by loud cannonading to the southwest, and the sky grew lurid with the flames of burning farmhouses and villages. Boisot had made the first bold move. Finding that the great dyke was but insufficiently guarded, he attacked it in the dead of night, at the same time setting fire to and ruining several adjacent strongholds of the enemy.

When morning dawned he was in possession of the coveted Land-scheiding without the loss of a single man. The discomfited Spaniards had but too late discovered their mistake in underestimating the courage of their assailants. A dove flew in on the morning of the eleventh, sent by Boisot, telling of the victory. Jacqueline carried it to the statehouse with the first feeling of enthusiasm she had experienced in many a long day. Perhaps the city really would be relieved, and perhaps Gysbert might be restored to them after all!

Chapter XI

Jacqueline Responds to an Urgent Summons

Since the great dyke had been pierced, an entire week had elapsed. Stout-hearted Admiral Boisot had expected to find the Land-scheiding the only barrier between his fleet and the city. But no sooner had this been passed than he discovered to his surprise and disgust that several more dykes and fortresses stood between himself and the goal. Three-quarters of a mile farther on was the "Green-way," another long dyke rising a foot above the water. But the Spaniards had not yet sufficiently learned their lesson, and this barrier also was very scantily guarded.

With his usual promptness and audacity, Boisot carried this situation, set his men to leveling the dyke, and the fleet passed through triumphantly. But again he was doomed to disappointment. Beyond the "Green-way" stretched a large, shallow lake called "Freshwater Mere," through which there was but one passage, a deep canal. As fortune would have it, however, this canal led directly under a bridge that was in possession of the Spaniards. This time the enemy had looked well to its defenses, and a few skirmishes soon convinced Boisot that the foe had the advantage of him. So he prudently drew off and waited.

Only two and a half miles from the beleaguered city lay the rescuing fleet, stranded in shallow water, unable to progress an inch. The east wind blew steadily, the waters decreased, and the Spaniards laughed in their faces. Within the city reigned a despair all the blacker for the brief illumination of hope that had now died. But God had not yet forsaken the cause of the right.

On the eighteenth of September, the wind changed, a great gale raged for three days out of the northwest, the waters rose rapidly, and the vessels were again afloat. Fortunately too, from some fugitives from one of the villages who had come aboard, Boisot learned of another course he could pursue, a little roundabout indeed, but having the advantage of avoiding the terrible, guarded bridge. He lost no time in availing himself of this, and the amazed Spaniards at the village of Nord Aa suddenly beheld this fear-inspiring flotilla bearing down upon them from an entirely unexpected direction. They fled precipitately, not even stopping to gather up their possessions, to the strongly fortified village of Zoeterwoude, only a mile and three-quarters from the city.

A little beyond Nord Aa, Boisot encountered the last dyke, the "Kirk-way." This he promptly leveled, but the wind had again changed, the water fell to the depth of only nine inches, and the fleet lay once more helpless in its shallows. Day by day passed and nothing occurred to alter the monotony of this inaction. But one circumstance took place which filled the Sea Beggars with renewed courage and inspired universal joy. The Prince of Orange, now recovered sufficiently from his long illness to be about, came on board the *Ark of Delft* to grasp the hand of the doughty Admiral. From thence he made a triumphal tour of all the vessels, instilling into every heart fresh courage, cheering, advising and directing. He looked pale and worn after his illness, and his devoted veterans, even these fierce Sea Beggars, were ready to fall at his feet and obey his lightest command. After a long and serious conference with Boisot, he returned to Delft.

Meanwhile, what of Jacqueline, upon the messages borne by whose carrier pigeons the whole city hung with breathless expectation? Since the passing of the Land-scheiding she had continued to carry constant messages to Van der Werf, for every time the admiral gained a new advantage, he hastened to dispatch another pigeon, for the encouragement of Leyden. Everyone who was not too weak with hunger to walk haunted the summit of Hengist Hill to watch the advance of the rescuers. It filled their hearts with new courage to note how small a space the besieging army was now forced to occupy—only a ring little more than a mile wide all about the city, with the threatening ocean and a crew of desperate Sea Beggars on one side and the hunger-maddened populace of Leyden in the center. The situation was certainly becoming a trifle embarrassing for the Spanish army!

Jacqueline occasionally went to Hengist Hill with Jan, who was now able to get about quite briskly. Dr. de Witt insisted that she must get out and take fresh air and exercise, and he was always willing to sit with Vrouw Voorhaas while she was away. They never allowed the girl to go far alone, for all yet feared the threat of Dirk Willumhoog to entrap her as well as her brother and took care that she was well guarded. Vrouw Voorhaas had also made decided improvement but was yet unable to leave her bed. The excessive weakness caused by her long self-denial and its consequences seemed almost impossible to overcome. Her constant inquiries about Gysbert, too, were becoming more and more difficult to answer, though they still kept up the fiction that he was quartered with Dr. de Witt during her illness. Sometimes it seemed as though she watched them all with hidden suspicion, and once she even murmured:

"I fear he is not safe! Something tells me he is in danger!" On the night when the fleet reached Nord Aa, a pigeon flew in bearing the tidings. Jacqueline found him, for she was constantly on the watch for messages, but since it was nearly nine o'clock, it was deemed best that Jan should carry the word to the burgomaster. The doctor had just left not five minutes before, and Jan hobbled off to execute his mission, leaving Jacqueline with Vrouw Voorhaas. The girl sat reading by the sickbed, casting an occasional glance at her patient, who was sound asleep. Presently, thinking she heard a knock at the door, she closed her book and hurried downstairs.

"'Tis early for Jan to be back," she thought. "He has but just left, and I know he will want to stay and chat awhile with Mynheer Van der Werf. Who can it be!" Some indefinable sensation of misgiving caused her to be a little long about opening the door. She was reassured, however, by seeing only a small boy who thrust a note into her hand and, turning, ran down the street. She called to him to come back, as there might be an answer required, but the child apparently did not hear her and was soon out of sight. Wonderingly she brought the scrap of paper to the candle-light and read its contents.

"*Juffrouw Jacqueline,*
If thou wouldst hear news of thy brother and dost also desire a chance to rescue him, I beg thee to come to the end of the Wirtemstrasse at once. Do not waste a moment, for the opportunity is but brief. The messenger there can only wait fifteen minutes. Thy brother sends his love.
One who is thy friend."

Jacqueline flushed with joy and then turned deathly pale. Hope, doubt, and distrust reigned equally in her mind. News of Gysbert!—a chance to rescue him!—she would go to the end of the world for that! But why had not the writer of the note signed his name? Why had the little boy who brought it run away so quickly? Oh, if Jan or Dr. de Witt were only here to advise her! Oh, if there were but more time! She glanced at the note again. It said, "Come immediately. The messenger has but fifteen minutes to wait." Fifteen minutes! *One* had gone already, while it would take at least ten to reach the appointed spot. Only four minutes in which to decide! But she had been forbidden to go out alone, especially at night. That, she concluded, would not interfere if they knew that Gysbert's welfare hung upon it. The girl was on a positive rack of torturing doubt, but the note again conquered. "Thy brother sends his love." Gysbert was then at least alive and safe, and was thinking of her? "One who is thy friend."—Surely, no one who wished her evil could subscribe that signature! If it were a *friend*, she need fear no harm. Then and there she formed her determination to risk all and obey this summons. God would surely watch over her!

Catching up a light wrap, she opened and closed the door softly and sped down the dark street. The night was starless and chilly; the few people she met were hurrying in the opposite direction to witness the conflagration at Nord Aa from Hengist Hill. Her way lay in the direction of the city wall between the Cow Gate and the Tower of Burgundy. It was a deserted section, and approaching it, she recognized it as the scene of Gysbert's adventure in the canal. A shudder of apprehension shook her, but she hurried on. It was do or die now, and nothing could have induced her to turn back.

Reaching the end of the Wirtemstrasse, she found herself at the bend of the canal described by Gysbert. A meadow stretched out before her, and beyond that rose a section of the grim wall of Leyden. There was not a soul in sight, and the girl began to think that in some way she had been deceived. Concluding, however, that she might possibly be a little ahead of time, she leaned over the rail of the stone bridge that crossed the canal and waited.

Suddenly, without a warning sound, she felt herself seized from behind. Before she could even cry out, a bandage was clapped over her mouth and fastened at the back of her head. Instantly another was bound over her eyes, and her hands were tied behind her in spite of her desperate struggles. In all this time she had not caught one glimpse of her captor, but she heard a rough voice mutter: "Ah!—I have thee at last! I have waited long enough for a chance to find thee unguarded by those two watchdogs!" And she knew it to be the voice of Dirk Willumhoog!

"Now walk with me and do exactly as I tell thee, if thou dost not wish to be knocked in the head!" the voice commanded in a low key. In utter despair Jacqueline was forced to obey, there being obviously no other course to pursue. The man grasped her by one arm and pulled her along after him. She could tell by the feeling of the ground that they were crossing the meadow, and anticipating what was to come, she trembled till her knees almost refused to support her. Presently she stepped up to her ankles in a pool of water.

"Draw a long breath and hold it!" commanded the voice. She

tried to do as she was told when with a sudden plunge she was immersed head and all for what seemed an interminable length of time. At last she felt her head raised above the surface. "Keep it up—so!" was the order. The icy current more than once forced her from her feet, causing her to slip under, and the atmosphere of the place struck a chill to her very marrow. Once again the ground gave way beneath her, and she felt the man's strong arm pulling her after him while he swam in water too deep for wading.

But the girl's senses could no longer stand the strain of cold, fatigue, and terror, and at this point she suddenly became unconscious. How the rest of the journey was accomplished she could never imagine, for she knew no more till she came to herself in what seemed to be some sort of narrow hallway. A door was opened and she was rudely thrust inside with the exclamation: "There!—At length!—I thought I should never get thee here!" Then the door was slammed to and loudly bolted.

Chapter XII

Reunited

For a time Jacqueline sat huddled and motionless in the corner where she had fallen. Her eyes were still bandaged, her mouth was gagged and her hands were tied behind her. She wondered vaguely whether they would ever come to release her from these bonds, and she shivered pitifully in her wet garments. Finally she roused herself and struggled feebly to free her hands. Her surprise was great when she found that the cords fell apart easily, but it was not till later that she guessed the secret—they had probably been severed nearly through before she was pushed into the room.

Once her hands were free, it was the work of but a few seconds to unbind her eyes and mouth and look about her. The room was in inky darkness, save where a small window admitted a faint gray light that indicated the outer world. There was no sound anywhere through the house. Oh, if they had only allowed her a little light! It was weird and uncanny to be thus thrust into a strange room and left there in utter darkness.

Presently the chill of her dripping clothes caused her to shudder and give an involuntary moan. A moment after she was electrified by hearing *something* move on the other side of the room. There was then some living thing in here with her! A chill, not of cold this time but of sheer terror, shook her from head to foot, and a wild desire to shriek aloud possessed her. Again the dreaded something moved, breathed hard, and uttered the word

"Jacqueline!" With a cry of joy and recognition she sprang across the room, and brother and sister found themselves tightly clasped in each other's arms. For a moment neither of them could do anything but sob and laugh and kiss the other distractedly. At last they grew sufficiently calm for speech.

"Oh, Gysbert, my brother! Art thou truly unharmed and well? How did this dreadful thing happen?" breathed Jacqueline.

"Yes, I am alive and whole," he replied, "but how I got here is a long story which I will tell thee later. But what about thee, Jacqueline? Thou art soaking wet! How didst thou come to be caught in the same trap?" In rapid sentences she sketched the history of the night's adventures.

"The scoundrel!" exclaimed Gysbert. "He must have brought thee through that same hole in the wall. I felt sure he had been planning to capture thee, but tonight when thou wert thrown so violently into the room, I could not tell whether it was thyself or some new trap he had been setting for me. Not till I heard thee moan was I sure. He has some deep-laid scheme in getting possession of us two, but what it is I cannot imagine. However, thou must get rid of these wet things, sister. There is a little room adjoining this where thou canst sleep. It has evidently been arranged for that purpose. Take off thy dripping clothes and wrap thyself in the bed-coverings, and we will then tell each other all that has happened since we parted.

"Now," said Gysbert, when his sister had arrayed herself in the warm bed-coverings, "I will begin by telling thee all about my journey to Rotterdam." And he rehearsed to her all the details of his interview with the Prince of Orange and continued: "It took me another day and night to pass Delft and reach the Spanish outposts. Feeling so certain I should get through in safety, I think I grew a little reckless and determined to try the route I had taken the first time. I never made a bigger mistake!

"In the first place, I hadn't an idea of the password, having been away three days. As luck would have it, I failed to encounter my friend Alonzo de Rova but did meet right face to face with the same captain who had arrested me before. He made short work of laying hands on me and delivered me over to the charge of about six or eight soldiers in a big tent. I tried again my scheme of drawing pictures, and they all became very much interested, hanging over me with laughter and much admiration as I drew the portrait of each one. I was hoping Alonzo would happen along, but he didn't.

"I cannot tell how my plan would have worked, nor whether the soldiers would have released me, for just as I was finishing the last one, I happened to look up, and there was the evil face of Dirk Willumhoog in the door of the tent staring down at me. I thought perhaps he would not recognize me in my disguise, but he did somehow. Disappearing for a moment, he came back with the captain and pointed to me, saying:

"'That is the boy I want, and I've been hunting for him all over. He is no Glipper at all, but a spy and a very dangerous character. Give him to me, and I'll see that he is properly taken care of.' I saw by this that resistance would be useless, so I very meekly followed him out of the tent. Once outside, he blindfolded my eyes, tied my hands, and led me what seemed a long distance. At last we entered this house. Upstairs we climbed, and inside this room he uncovered my eyes. 'We'll see if thou art a Glipper!' he said, and he proceeded to wash off all the stain. 'Now we will pay off some old scores of long standing!' he added, and with a heavy switch, he gave me such a beating as I never had in my life before."

"He beat *thee*!" exclaimed the girl, her eyes blazing in the dark. "Oh, I could kill him for it!"

"Yes, but I did not cry out!" replied Gysbert proudly. "Not one moan did he hear from me, till at last he stopped from sheer weariness. 'That's to pay for thy kind remarks on the day I left Leyden!' he said. 'We will settle the rest later!' Then he took my bag and examined it, wondering at the herbs and finding the food and pigeon. 'What hast thou here?' he asked. 'And why wast thou outside the walls?' I told him we were hungry, and I had been trying to get some food by selling herbs. 'Thou liest!' he shouted. 'What was this carrier pigeon for? I tell thee thou carriest messages to the enemy!' "I said I had taken it so that in case I could not get back in time, I could send a message. 'Well, *I'll* send the message,' he replied, 'and it will be somewhat differently worded, thou canst wager!' What was it, Jacqueline?" The girl told him, and both together puzzled over the supposition that Dirk and Vrouw Voorhaas must sometime have met and held some secret knowledge in common. She also told him what the woman had uttered in her delirium, but they could make nothing of the mystery. Then Gysbert went on with his story.

"After that he left me, bolting the door behind him, and I was free to look about me and see where I was, as far as my limited space would permit. I found myself in this room which thou wilt see at daylight, with the other small one opening from it. Both contained a bed, and that made me guess that at some time he hoped to capture thee also. There are two little windows well guarded by heavy iron bars like a prison. However, I could see enough through them to guess where I was. This is a little, lonely farmhouse well outside the village of Zoeterwoude. Thou knowest where that is, Jacqueline. We have often gone there to buy pigeons. It is about a mile and a half from Leyden.

"The walls and floorings of the rooms are thick, and I seldom hear any sounds from the rest of the house. There is no fireplace and very little furniture. Well, here I was, and likely to remain till fortune again turned in my favor! For three successive days Dirk came up and gave me a beating, till I foresaw that this was to become a daily practice. Otherwise I had food enough shoved in the door at me—more than I had in Leyden!—and nothing on earth to do. At length I became thoroughly weary of the beating performance and hit upon a scheme to avoid it. And what dost thou think that was, Jacqueline?"

"I cannot guess!" she answered.

"Why, I pretended I had the *plague!*" he cried gleefully. "Oh, Jacqueline, thou canst not guess what a desperate coward that Dirk Willumhoog is! One day when I heard him coming, I held my breath till I was scarlet in the face, like fever. I lay covered up in bed, and when he entered, I began to toss my arms about and rave, as though light in the head. He did not beat me that time, but stared at me uneasily for a while and went out muttering. He did not come in again that day, and I had a chance to make myself a little worse!

"I found a place in the wall where some loose plaster had fallen away from the brick lining within. Breaking off some of this brick, powdering and moistening it, I thus obtained some fine red paint with which I proceeded to decorate myself. With the pail of water for a mirror, all over my face and hands I imitated the blotches that appear on the plague-stricken. Oh, I must have been a fine, healthful sight!

"When Dirk came in to visit me next morning, he looked, gave one howl, and rushed out of the room! I have not seen him since, and I know he believes me far gone in this illness. Strange to say though, in spite of his hatred, he does not seem to wish me to die, but has caused to be thrust in the door the finest food and nourishment that could be procured. I could live like a lord if I wished, but I scarcely touch it, saving only enough to keep life in me, else he would surely suspect. Thus have I passed the three weeks!" He ceased to speak, and for a while they sat silent, hoping, doubting, fearing for the future, yet rejoicing that they were at last together.

"But now thou must go to bed, Jacqueline," said Gysbert at length. "Thou art wearied out and sleep will do thee good." Obediently she crept into the bed in the little room, dropped asleep almost as soon as her head touched the pillow, and never woke till the sun was streaming in at the small window high overhead. Rising and donning the clothes that were now dry, she hurried into the next room to get the first glimpse at her brother.

He was indeed a remarkable sight as he lay in bed exhibiting his horribly blotched face and hands. It would have taken a keen eye, so cleverly had he executed this dreadful decoration, to detect it as false.

"Thou must pretend to be greatly alarmed about me, Jacqueline, should they interview thee, and do not be surprised at my ravings, for they are right hair-raising!" Gysbert had hardly uttered this caution when there was a sound of steps approaching the door. Immediately he began to toss his arms about, moan, mutter, and occasionally shriek in a muffled manner.

"Go away! Go away from me!" he raved. "Thou art not my sister! Why dost thou say thou art Jacqueline! I do not know thee! Thou art someone sent by that enemy of ours! Go away, go away, I tell thee!" Then the door was unbolted, a basket of food was thrust within, and a voice was heard calling above the racket of Gysbert's pretended delirium:

"Juffrouw Jacqueline! Is thy brother very ill?"

"Yes," answered the girl trembling. "He is so sorely ill that I fear he will die!"

"Well, thou must not let him die! Thou must nurse him carefully. We do not wish either of you to come to harm."

"Why dost thou keep us here?" demanded Jacqueline, growing bolder. "Let us go away where he can get a doctor and proper treatment."

"'Tis not for thee to inquire why thou art here. That thou shalt perhaps know in due time," answered the voice. "As for a doctor, it is impossible to procure one and inadvisable to bring him here if we could. Thou knowest much about nursing the plague and hast had rare experience in the city. If thou dost need any special food or medicine for him, we will try to procure it, but otherwise all must remain as it is. Dost think this case is very contagious?"

"Ah, very!" replied Jacqueline, slyly. "Even the odor from the room is enough to infect one, especially if one fears it greatly!" At this the door was slammed hastily shut, and when the children had heard the last departing footsteps of Dirk Willumhoog die away, they could not, in spite of their danger, repress a giggle of uncontrollable mirth!

Chapter XIII

Adrian Van der Werf

Words cannot express the astonishment of Jan Van Buskirk when he returned from the burgomaster's to find no Jacqueline in the little house in Belfry Lane. Unfortunately, she had still grasped the crumpled note in her hand when she left the house, so he had absolutely no clue to her whereabouts. The only explanation he could offer to himself was that she must have gone out unpremeditatedly to obtain some fresh medicine at a little chemist shop nearby. So he sat down to wait for her return.

But the time passed on and still she did not come. An hour rolled by and Vrouw Voorhaas awoke to ask for Jacqueline. Jan quieted her by telling her that the girl had retired to take a little rest, and Vrouw Voorhaas went to sleep again. Another hour passed, and Jan, frightened almost out of his senses, resolved to seek Dr. de Witt. Waking Vrouw Voorhaas, he told her that he did not feel well and was going out to consult the doctor. She, he said, must go quietly to sleep again, as it was nothing serious. Unsuspectingly she assented, and he hurried out to find Dr. de Witt, weary with his day's exertion, just about to turn into bed. The tale was soon told, and Pieter de Witt lost not a moment in resuming his clothes.

"She has answered some summons," said he, "and has been led into a trap. I know it! I have suspected all along that something like this would happen when we least dreamed of it. It is unthinkable!" From end to end the two searched the city that night. No one had heard of her, none had seen her, and they returned home in the gray of early morning, footsore, despairing, and heartsick.

"It will kill Vrouw Voorhaas," said De Witt, "and by this time she must certainly know something is wrong, since both you and the girl have been away all night. Come right for me, Jan, if it is necessary, but I must turn in now for just a few moments' rest, or I'll break down too." Poor Jan crept home broken and almost in tears. At the door he was met by Vrouw Voorhaas, who had dragged herself out of bed to search the house for its usual inmates. Her eyes were wild and haggard, and she faced him fiercely.

"Where hast thou been all night? Where are Jacqueline and Gysbert?" she demanded.

"Oh, they are all right—all safe!" he tried to prevaricate, but his face betrayed him.

"It is not so! Thou liest!" she interrupted him. "Evil has come to them—I know it! I know it! For many days have I suspected that all was not well with Gysbert, and now Jacqueline has disappeared too. Thou canst not deceive me! Do not try! Ah, Dirk Willumhoog, thou—" She could not finish but fell unconscious at the feet of Jan.

He tried to raise her, but in his own weakened condition found it impossible and concluded that the best thing to do was to go back at once for the doctor. Pieter de Witt, exhausted but indefatigable still in the cause of his friends, hurried back with him at once. Together they succeeded in raising her and getting her back to bed, but they failed utterly in restoring her to consciousness. Dr. de Witt shook his head many times over the black prospect.

"This shock has caused a sudden relapse—and no wonder!" he said. "I sadly fear that the end is not now far away. Thou wilt have to be her attendant now, Jan. For the sake of the children do thy best, and I will help thee!"

"There is one more possibility that we have not tried," said Jan. "We did not go to the burgomaster's. Can it be possible that another message came while I was returning, and she hurried out with it, going some other way? Perchance as it was late, Mynheer Van der Werf's wife would not allow her to go home and has kept her till morning. Perchance she has been taken sick there."

"It is a small chance, Jan—a very small one!" said De Witt. "They would surely have sent us word in any case. But go to him if it will set thy heart at rest. I will stay with Vrouw Voorhaas the while." Jan set out once more, his poor old legs fairly tottering under him with loss of sleep, lack of food, and weakness. But excitement still buoyed him up, and the faint, vague hope that Jacqueline might have passed the night with Mevrouw Van der Werf spurred him on to one more effort. It was yet too early to find the burgomaster at the statehouse, so he proceeded straight to the residence in the Werfsteg.

He was obliged to lift the heavy knocker several times before he could arouse the sleepy servants within. At length he was admitted by a yawning, hastily clad domestic who went to call the burgomaster. Van der Werf came down quickly, expecting another message from outside the city. His face was pale, haggard, and careworn, and his eyes showed plainly that he had passed a sleepless night.

"Jan," he cried, "what news hast thou? Is there another message?" Then seeing the old man's wild, questioning eyes, "Ah! What ails thee? Has anything dreadful happened?"

"Is she not here? Is she not here?" muttered Jan, sinking limply into a chair.

"Is who not here?" questioned Van der Werf mystified.

"Jacqueline! The Juffrouw Jacqueline!"

"Juffrouw Jacqueline has not been here for three days! Why, Jan, what has happened?" Then the old man told the story while Van der Werf listened with darkening face.

"'Tis passing strange! 'Tis fairly devilish!" he vociferated. "I could feel no worse if harm had come to one of my own family! Nay, I know nothing about her, and what is worse, I can do nothing. I am as helpless as thou art. My hands are tied! Thou sayest thou hast searched the city? Even I can do no more! If she has by any means been taken beyond the walls—Heaven help her!" The two men sat for some moments, gloomily silent. Jan had reached a point of exhaustion where his body absolutely refused to obey the behests of his mind—when he attempted to take his departure, he could not rise from his chair.

"Thou must stay and have a little food and drink—such poor stuff as I can offer thee!" said the burgomaster, seeing his plight, and he rang for a servant to bring in such fare as they had in the house. Jan had no heart to attack the breakfast, but Van der Werf insisted that he should eat a little to sustain his strength. So he made a brave attempt, while the burgomaster strode restlessly up and down the room.

"Jan, Jan!" he cried at length. "The Lord hath put more on my shoulders than mortal man can bear! Dost thou know, it is by my will alone that this city holds out? Daily I receive the most cajoling and fair-spoken notes from Commander Valdez. He makes the most extravagant promises of mercy and leniency if I will only open the gates. 'Tis but a siren's song, as everyone well knows! Yet the dissatisfied ones are clamorous to try once more the mercy of the Spaniard!—They accuse me of starving and killing them for a mere question of my personal pride. Has not one of my own family already died of the plague? Is not my own wife even now desperately ill? Am *I* the gainer by my policy? Alas, no! Jan, a dead body was found placed against my door yesterday morning. We all know what that means—they lay the city's terrible plight to my stubbornness. But while I live, I swear I will not open the gates!"

When Jan, somewhat refreshed, had finished his meal and rose to start for home, Van der Werf offered to accompany him a way, saying he wanted no breakfast himself and must be at the statehouse early. Together they went out, the burgomaster supporting the old man's feeble steps as tenderly as a son might have assisted his father. Not many rods behind them, two or three malcontents, well-known for having always leaned toward the opinions of the Glippers, began to follow the magistrate, muttering remarks of no very pleasant nature. Jan the fiery turned about once and rebuked them:

"Hold thy tongue, Janus de Vries! And thou, Pieter Brouwer, hast thou not thyself been fed from the burgomaster's own kitchen? I know all about thee! Who art thou to utter complaint?"

"Do not pay any more attention to them, Jan, lest they begin to be wordy and attract more attention to themselves and us than is desirable!" said Van der Werf. But a crowd had already begun to gather, which in an incredibly short time grew into a mob, shouting, yelling, gesticulating, fiercely demanding bread and the opening of the gates. The burgomaster began to fear, not for his own life, but for that of the feeble old man, who would be so helpless in their hands did they come at last to violence. Just at this crisis, they emerged into the triangular space in front of the old church of St. Pancras.

Deeming the time ripe for him to exert all his powers of persuasion on this threatening throng, Van der Werf ascended the steps of the edifice, placed Jan in a protecting angle of the doorway, and turned about to face the crowd. As he removed his great felt hat, the morning sunlight fell through the surrounding lime trees on a face, calm, imposing, and softened with a great and overwhelming sadness. Its silent appeal touched even the hearts of the famishing mob, and when he raised his hand there was instant silence. Then after a moment he spoke in words that history has forever made memorable:

"What would ye, my friends? Why do ye murmur that we do not break our vows and surrender to the Spaniards? That would be a fate more horrible than what the city now endures! I tell you I have made an oath to hold the city, and may God give me strength to keep that oath! I can die but once, whether by your hands, or the enemy's, or the hand of God. My own fate is indifferent to me, but not so that of the city which has been entrusted to my care. I know that we shall starve if we are not soon relieved, but starvation is preferable to a dishonored death, is it not? Your threats move me not! My life is at your disposal. Here is my sword— plunge it into my breast if ye will! Take my body to appease your hunger, but do not expect me to surrender while I live!" He held out his arms a moment, then dropped them at his side. Instantly a great shout of approval went up from the multitude. In the twinkling of an eye the threats were changed to cries of encouragement to the city and defiance to the enemy, transmuted by the persistent, dogged courage of one man standing absolutely alone!

"Long live Adrian Van der Werf!" they shouted. "We will indeed fight to the end!" And leaving the two standing on the steps of St. Pancras, the crowd rushed to the walls, where they remained all day hurling renewed defiance at the Spaniards.

When the mob had deserted them, Van der Werf escorted Jan to Belfry Lane and left him at the door, after which he proceeded with firmer step and easier mind to his daily duties at the statehouse. But when Jan reached Vrouw Voorhaas's room, he sat suddenly down in a chair and looked hard at the doctor, who noticed that the old man's expression was as exalted as though he had seen some heavenly vision.

"What is the matter?" he asked. "Hast thou found Juffrouw Jacqueline?"

"Nay," answered Jan, "I have not found her. But Pieter de Witt, I have just beheld the finest act of courage that it was ever the lot of one poor man to witness! If Adrian Van der Werf can thus bear the sorrows of a whole city on his heart, thou and I, through God, must not shrink at the burdens His wisdom has seen fit to lay upon us!" And he told the doctor of his morning's experience.

Chapter XIV

Alonzo de Rova Is as Good as His Word

Meanwhile, Jacqueline and Gysbert, isolated in the upper room of the little farmhouse in Zoeterwoude, found themselves with a great deal of time on their hands and liberty to do pretty much as they liked within their limited space. The fiction of Gysbert's illness with the plague was rigorously adhered to, and beyond opening the door a crack to poke in the food, Dirk Willumhoog never ventured to intrude. Every day he would shout through the closed door to Jacqueline, inquiring about Gysbert's condition. Generally she would reply that he was no better, or that the symptoms were very much worse. Very infrequently she answered that he was a little better.

They lived on the best of fare, for Dirk was evidently anxious that the patient should have every opportunity in that way to improve. Gysbert now ate even more than his share, but Jacqueline was of course supposed to have consumed the larger amount. On the whole, though, they felt that the deception could not be sustained very much longer without discovery. From the barred windows they watched constantly, endeavoring to discover in that way, if possible, something that was going on. There was little life about the farmhouse, though they occasionally saw a few Spanish soldiers go in and out and a woman sometimes moving about the yard. Only once they overheard a conversation that threw some light on whose house they were inhabiting. A soldier entered the yard one day and was accosted by this woman who seemed to belong to the place.

"Hast thou heard any news of my husband?" she questioned.

"Nothing certain, Vrouw Hansleer," he replied, "but there is a rumor that the Prince has discovered him and had him cast into prison." Then the two passed out of hearing. But Gysbert snapped his fingers delightedly and cried:

"*Hansleer*, is it! Now I know where we are, Jacqueline! The Prince told me that the name of the wretch who was deceiving him was Joachim Hansleer—dost thou not remember? And it is due to me that he has been imprisoned! How much dost thou suppose our lives would be worth if Dirk Willumhoog and Vrouw Hansleer knew that! Long live the Prince, and may he keep our secret!"

But one day when Gysbert was looking from the window, he was startled by the sight of a figure that had something familiar in its aspect. It was a man in the uniform of a Spanish soldier who was tall and finely built, but his face could not be seen by the boy. Presently however, he looked up, and Gysbert recognized in an instant the features of Alonzo de Rova! Immediately a plan formed itself in his mind.

"Jacqueline," he whispered, "it is a big risk, but I'm going to take the chance! He half-promised to help me if ever I needed it. Now we will see! The yard is deserted, and I will try to attract his attention." Suiting the action to the word, he gave a low whistle, and the soldier looked up. Seeing this strange, horribly spotted face at the window, he uttered a startled exclamation:

"By St. Lawrence! What dost thou want with me? Art thou the plague-stricken boy Dirk Willumhoog is keeping for some unknown purpose?"

"Yes," answered Gysbert in a low tone. "Dost thou not remember the little Glipper lad who drew thy portrait?"

"By the Pope! I do!" replied Alonzo. "Surely thou art not he!"

"I am," said Gysbert. "Wilt thou help me? If so, ask to come up and see me."

"But thou hast the plague!" answered the soldier. For reply

Gysbert shook his head and significantly rubbed off one of the brick-dust spots. Alonzo gave a loud guffaw of appreciation at the joke and nodded encouragingly. "Wait!" he motioned with his lips, for someone was coming out of the house. Not long after, the children heard a great commotion on the stairs. Immediately Gysbert leaped into bed, covered himself well, and began to moan and rave incoherently, while Jacqueline trembled lest their secret should now be discovered through her brother's rashness. Nearer and nearer came the sounds, as of remonstrance and scuffling combined:

"I tell thee I will see them, Dirk! It will do no harm, and thou sayest the lass is pretty. I wager five florins she is not so fair as my sweetheart in Madrid! Dost thou take the wager?"

"Nay, but thou wilt catch the plague! Thou canst not wish to risk that. The boy is a terrible sight, and the very odor of the room will infect thee!"

"Truly man! How careful thou art of my health! But, fortunately, I do not fear the plague. I had it three years ago and got over it bravely. They say one is then exempt and can never catch it again. Let me go, Dirk."

"Aye, but I will not answer for the consequences, thou reckless man!" answered Dirk as he reluctantly unbolted the door, shutting it again quickly when the soldier was once inside. Alonzo sat down on a vacant chair and laughed till the tears rolled down his cheeks at the capers Gysbert cut, raving and tossing, shouting and groaning, and flinging the bedclothes about.

"Thou art the cleverest lad I ever met!" he whispered, glancing significantly at the door to intimate that Dirk was probably outside listening. Then aloud:

"By the Pope! Thou art in a right bad predicament, and methinks thou hast not much longer to survive, my lively boy! And thy sister is truly as handsome as Dirk painted her. But I like the dark beauty of my Inez best!" Here someone called Dirk loudly, and they heard him descending the stairs. Knowing, however, that his absence would probably not be for long, they made the best use of their time.

"De Rova," hurriedly whispered Gysbert, "we are caught here like rats in a trap! Canst thou help us to escape?"

"Willingly would I," answered the soldier, "for I have not forgotten the splendid portrait of me which I sent to Madrid. I do truly think it has at last turned the undecided heart of fair Inez Montagno toward me, for her letters of late have been warmer and less flouting. Also I bear no particular love to Dirk Willumhoog, who has done me one or two sneaking ill turns that he thinks I do not trace to him. But how can I aid thee? I cannot unlock doors so carefully guarded. I cannot waft thee from barred windows, nor can I rescue thee with ladders! What wilt thou?"

"Only one thing!" said Gysbert quickly. "Hast thou a knife about thee? If so, leave it with me, I pray! No—" seeing the soldier's questioning glance—"I do not mean to kill anyone with it, but with something sharp in our possession I think we can furnish our own means of escape." For an answer the Spaniard drew from his belt a short-handled weapon with a strong Toledo blade and placed it in the boy's hands. Quickly concealing it under his mattress, Gysbert thanked him with an eloquent look. But footsteps were again approaching, and all knew that the interview must soon end. Alonzo turned to Jacqueline with a look of reverent admiration in his eyes:

"Fair young Juffrouw, beyond everything do I admire thy quiet courage and devotion to thy brother. For the sake of my lady, Doña Inez Montagno, whom I shall one day tell all about thee, may I kiss thy hand in farewell?" Jacqueline, genuinely touched, extended her hand. De Rova dropped gallantly on one knee and touched it with his lips.

"I would that I could do more for thee," he whispered, "but I have done all that is in my power. God bless you both and grant you success!" A knock was heard at the door, Gysbert began to rave again, and Alonzo prepared to take his departure.

"They are hard put to it!" the children heard him telling Dirk as he went out. "I doubt whether the boy will recover, and he is not in his senses a minute. But I have won my wager, Dirk! I consider

Doña Inez far handsomer than thy little Juffrouw Jacqueline in there!"

"But is he not a jewel!" whispered Gysbert. "I told thee I had made a friend when I cultivated his acquaintance. This pretty little blade is going to save us, I hope!" And he stroked the weapon admiringly.

"But how?" demanded Jacqueline, in wonder.

"Trust me, and thou wilt see!" was all he would reply.

Chapter XV

The Eavesdroppers and the Plot

Gysbert did not keep his sister long in doubt as to the use he proposed to make of Alonzo de Rova's Toledo blade. The first thing he did caused her considerable wonder and not a little alarm. In one corner of the room he pried up the tiles of the flooring for the space of a square foot and cut away the planking underneath, leaving nothing but some thin lath and plaster between them and the room below.

"Oh, Gysbert! What art thou doing?" asked Jacqueline in distress. "We will be discovered and all will be lost!"

"Not at all!" said Gysbert as he covered up his work by carefully replacing everything he had removed. "No one will suspect what I have done, and through this hole we can listen to much that goes on below. We may hear something worthwhile if we listen hard enough! But that is only one thing I intend to do with this valuable weapon. Let me show thee to what other use it may be put!" He went to the window, reconnoitered long and carefully to see that no one was near, and then commenced to file away at one of the iron bars, digging carefully into the wood in which it was imbedded and using every effort to dislodge it from the socket in which it was set.

"This will be a long and tedious piece of work," he remarked. "There are three thick bars, each set stoutly in woodwork nearly as hard as iron itself, and we want to do this work so carefully that it will not be noticeable should anyone enter the room. Each bar will have to be loosened both top and bottom, and I know not how long it will take us. We will work as constantly as we can, and I doubt not in time we shall be free as the birds, as far as this window is concerned. 'Tis a good thing the blade is sharp and enduring!"

"Yes, but even so," demurred Jacqueline, "what are we going to do when the bars are loosed? To be as free as the birds, as thou sayest, we must have wings, for we are fully twenty feet from the ground!"

"There are many ways to get out of a window, Jacqueline, as thou wouldst know if thou hadst climbed in and out of one as many times as I have! But that too will all come in good season, and meanwhile we must work away at the bars." Hope—even vague and indefinite hope—lends wings to the soul and zest to the brain and hands. This faint glimmer that had been cast across the blackness of the two children's prospects so filled their hearts with its brightness that they were almost gay as they sawed away on the stout iron bars. They would have shouted and sung, had not that performance surely encouraged unwelcome attention in their direction.

That same night Gysbert removed the tiles and piece of plank from the hole he had dug in the flooring. Leaning over it, the children strove to gather, from any sounds they might hear, what was going on beneath them. It was destined that they should hear something that night which, while it enlightened them upon several points hitherto inscrutable, served in no way to add to their peace of mind. The room just under theirs was evidently one that was not often used, for it seemed to be dark and deserted. Presently however, a light shone through the cracks in the ceiling, someone was heard moving about, and voices whispered words that could not be distinguished. At length the sentence "He is even now coming!" penetrated up through the ceiling, and there was another silence. Then the neighing of horses was heard outside. A loud tramping of heavily shod feet resounded on the wooden floors, the door of the room below opened, and three people entered.

"Sit you down! Pray, sit you down!" said a voice easily recognized as Dirk Willumhoog's. "We will be secure here from all interruption and can talk freely, with absolutely no fear of being overheard!" Here Gysbert pinched Jacqueline till she almost laughed aloud. Two gruff voices replied in monosyllables, and there was a scraping of chairs and jingling of spurs as the two horsemen placed themselves at the table.

"Now," commanded one of the gruff voices, "tell us quickly, Dirk Willumhoog, what is this plan that thou hast, and we will then discuss whether it be worth considering!"

"Nay, nay, Commander Valdez!" whined Dirk. "We must not be quite so speedy!"

"Didst thou hear that, Jacqueline?" whispered Gysbert. "Commander Valdez!—Now we are going to hear something worthwhile!"

"Come, come!" put in the third voice impatiently. "Why all this parleying? If thou hast a plan worth considering, out with it, and thou shalt be recompensed accordingly. Dost thou think us willing to sit here all night to split hairs with such as thou?"

"Not so fast! Not so fast, Colonel Borgia!" complained Dirk. "If my plan is worth anything, it is worth bargaining for, and I do not intend to sell it cheaply, I assure you!"

"Jacqueline," again whispered Gysbert, "there is some dreadful plan afoot! Colonel Borgia is the Spaniard in command of Fort Lammen, the strongest redoubt against the city. Listen!—"

"Well, Dirk," interrupted Valdez, perceiving evidently that it would not do to try bullying this subtle rascal, "tell us then, what is thy price for the service thou dost propose to render the Spanish army?"

"Fifty thousand florins!" replied Dirk, calmly but firmly.

"*Fifty thousand flying devils!*" roared Valdez, pounding the table with his fist. "Dost thou think the Spanish treasury is a mine of diamonds? Away with thee, thou scurvy rascal! Come, Borgia! 'Tis useless parleying with a madman!"

"Gentlemen," remarked Dirk, quite unmoved by this outburst on the part of the Spanish general, "you do me wrong. Did you but know my plan, you would say it was easily worth full twice the amount I have named. However, I have other ways of disposing profitably of my secret, should my terms not appeal to you!" In the silence that ensued, the two listeners could imagine the Spaniards consulting each other with uncertain glances. At last the voice of Valdez spoke again, this time in a more conciliatory tone:

"Willumhoog, I am not authorized to offer any such amount as thou dost name. But I swear to thee that I will consult with one ever gracious and merciful King Philip II at the earliest opportunity to obtain this amount for thee, using every influence in my power."

"Will Your Worship put that down in writing?" inquired Dirk eagerly.

"Certainly, certainly!" replied the general, glad to have made an impression so easily. Dirk hastened out, evidently to obtain pen and paper, and was back again in a jiffy. "I have one more request to make," he remarked in honeyed tones.

"As thou wilt!" said Valdez.

"It is that Your Worship will write at my dictation."

There was another uneasy pause, and then the general acquiesced, muttering that he did not have to write anything that he did not wish!

"I, General Valdez," dictated Dirk, "Commander of the Spanish army before Leyden, do hereby give my promise that I will intercede with His Majesty, Philip II, to pay over to Dirk Willumhoog for the valuable secret he shall impart concerning an unknown entrance into the city the sum of fifty thousand florins." Scratch, scratch went the pen, and coming to this point, Valdez exclaimed: "There now I will sign my name!"

"Not quite yet!" said Dirk quietly. "There is something else!"— "And if I do not succeed in so persuading His Majesty, I stand ready to reimburse said Dirk Willumhoog for the amount remaining above what he shall have already received, out of my own private funds and estates."

"Never!" shouted Valdez, springing to his feet and clanking around the room. "Dost thou take me for a natural-born fool, thou sneaking rascal!"

"The loss will be all Your Worship's," responded Dirk, unmoved, "as the glory would also be, could you but take the city by surprise. I am not asking for glory. I do not wish my part in it to become generally known. All I ask is the gold!" Valdez and Borgia consulted together for a moment in low tones, and the result of their consultation seemed to be the hasty decision that they must capitulate.

"Very well!" declared the general. "I will write as thou hast said, but mark my words! Thou hadst better keep out of my way, Dirk Willumhoog, when this transaction is completed!"

"And now, gentlemen, just one thing more," added Dirk when the writing was finished and in his possession. "As an earnest of your good faith, I require a thousand florins to be paid me at once!" More splutterings from Borgia and explosions from Valdez ensued, but this was evidently mere bluster, for after a due amount of bickering and bargaining, a clinking of coins was heard, and money was counted out slowly and reluctantly.

"There!" said Valdez, "Thou hast now every jot thou didst demand. Out with thy secret, and be quick about it, for we have not all night to spend!"

"This, then, is my story," answered Dirk. "I have discovered—never mind how!—a passageway through a certain part of the wall of Leyden. Not a soul knows of its existence save myself, and none could ever find it unassisted, for I myself stumbled upon it quite by chance. There is room for but one to pass through at a time, and the passage is dangerous. But it would be an easy matter to introduce a regiment of soldiers through it in the night, and in the morning the town would be yours, for the inhabitants are all too weak from starvation to make much resistance."

"But where *is* this secret passage?" demanded Valdez.

"That will I not divulge till I lead the first soldier through it," replied Willumhoog shrewdly. "When does Your Worship think would be the best and earliest opportunity to effect the entrance?"

Again Valdez and Borgia consulted together.

"Today is the thirtieth of September," replied the general. "On the night of October third, we will have all in readiness, and thou shalt fulfill thy promise. At the same time, Colonel Borgia shall make an assault upon the wall on the opposite side of the city and thus draw off the attention from our place of ingress." With a few more remarks relative to the payment of the money, and a hasty and anything but cordial leave-taking, the two Spaniards tramped out, mounted their horses and rode away. The lights in the room below were extinguished, the door was shut, and darkness and silence reigned throughout the farmhouse. But up in their prison room, the two children clasped each other and shuddered with horror at the dark crime that was soon to be committed.

"It is frightful, Gysbert!" moaned Jacqueline. "Our beautiful city that has so long and so bravely held out will be given over by this traitor to the Spanish fury!"

"But what makes me feel the worst," raged Gysbert, "is that I could not warn the burgomaster of that breach, as the Prince bade me! Why did I not think to tell Mynheer Van der Werf before I went away! Why didst not thou tell him, Jacqueline?"

"I somehow never thought of it when I was with him, and he never asked me how Dirk got in. I think his mind was all but distracted with the burden of the city's distress so that he could give no heed to what seemed then but a comparatively light matter. Oh, Gysbert! Can we do nothing about it? Surely God who led us to overhear this vile plot will show us the way to foil it!"

"I think He will!" said Gysbert reverently. "And anyhow, I am going to pray tonight that He show us some means of getting out of our prison and warning the city. Wilt thou too, Jacqueline?"

"I will indeed!" answered the girl. "And before we go to bed we will work long at the bars, for that seems our surest means of escape."

"Only three days!" groaned Gysbert. "I would that it were as many times as far away. But in three days we can do much—if we work hard!"

Chapter XVI

When the Wind Changed

All the next day the children bent every effort toward sawing and digging away at their window bars, but the hours wore away and only one had been completely loosened, while another was unfastened at the bottom. The knife-blade was becoming dull with this rough usage, and their courage dropped in proportion as their strength gave out and night approached. Well on in the afternoon, Gysbert again removed the tiles and planking, for both had imagined they heard unusual sounds in the room below. They were not mistaken. A moment's listening convinced them that it was Dirk and the wife of Joachim Hansleer, holding an animated conversation in low tones.

"Give me my share now, Dirk!" they heard the woman say. "If thou art going to depart for Spain shortly, it will be just as well to settle up this matter at once. I know not where my good man Joachim is, nor when I will see him again, and I need the money."

"I shall not depart for Spain with those brats till after the sack of the city, when the boy ought to be better. I do not half believe he is as ill as he makes out to be. Why canst thou not wait till then?" answered Dirk. "I must go away this afternoon and will probably not be back till after the third. I am going to make one more test to see if my secret is still safe and practicable. When I return will be time enough!"

"Thou art a slippery eel, Dirk Willumhoog, and that I know

right well!" replied the woman. "After the excitement is all over, thou wouldst find some means of sliding away without paying up thy just debts. I swear to thee that if thou dost not pay me at once those three hundred florins which are due me for my trouble, I will go straightway upstairs after thou art gone to the city and release those two children! And I care not what may be the consequences!"

This knockdown argument evidently convinced Dirk that it would be best to parley no longer with the decided Vrouw Hansleer, but pay her at once. There was a clinking of coins, a counting aloud, several disputes over the reckoning, and at last the matter was settled and peace restored.

"Remember," warned Dirk as they were leaving the room, "to guard those children well, for they will surely mean more money to us—" Then the door was shut and the listeners heard no more.

"What can all this mean!" queried Gysbert. "Didst thou hear him speak of 'taking those two brats to Spain in a short time'? That means us, of course! What can he possibly mean to do with us there, and how can we bring him more money? One would think we were important personages and he was trying to get a ransom for us!"

"It is all dark and mysterious," answered his sister, "but if we do what we hope, Master Willumhoog will receive a little surprise before October third! Come, we must waste no more time, but work away!" Later on they saw Dirk Willumhoog leave the house, carrying with him a bag which they did not doubt contained the remaining seven hundred florins. While watching his progress down the road, Gysbert's attention suddenly became fixed on something in the sky, and he seized Jacqueline's arm excitedly.

"Look, look!" he cried. "Dost thou see?"

"I see nothing! What is it?"

"Why, the wind is changing! Look at those black clouds rising out of the northwest! Look at the leaves of the trees all bending toward the east! Look at the birds flying so low! I tell thee, Jacqueline, we are going to have a terrible storm! The equinoctial gale should have come a week ago, but it is here at last!"

What Gysbert predicted was quite correct. The continual east wind had at last shifted to the northwest, bringing with it the strong salt smell of the sea. The sky was still beautifully clear and blue, but a weather-wise person would have certainly read the signs of coming change. Dirk Willumhoog was now far out of sight, but they saw Vrouw Hansleer come out to the yard and scan the horizon anxiously.

"Here, Jacqueline," said Gysbert when the woman had gone in, "give me that knife now, while thou dost take a rest. We must get along even faster, for if the wind holds and the water rises, there will be fine doings tonight, and we want to be prepared to take our part. Look! I think the top of this end bar will give way in a short time."

"This surely will float the fleet, will it not?" asked his sister. "The night I was captured, Boisot sent a message that he was at Nord Aa but must remain there until the water rose. They have probably been stranded there ever since."

"Surely, surely!" answered Gysbert. "And what is more, we ought to have a full view from our little window here if they come by. For though we are a good distance from the canal, I think we could get a fine sight of a battle, if there is to be one. Oh, I hope there will be a battle!" In a frenzy of excitement, they kept at their work till darkness fell. Before the last streaks of twilight had faded, they had witnessed the puddles in the road grow and spread into small ponds, the ponds widen and join themselves into a shallow lake which lapped against the walls of the house.

Then came the tempest! The wind raged and howled; the sky was black with high-piled clouds; the tree branches tossed and groaned or were split asunder with loud cracking noises; the walls of the farmhouse shook, the windows rattled, and pandemonium itself seemed let loose! The children trembled, half with awed admiration at this war in the elements, half with delight at what this would mean to the besieged city, and clasped their hands convulsively at every louder roar of the wind or crash of huge trees falling. Down below it was evident that panic and disorder reigned supreme. Cries and shouts of dismay mingled with the shrill screaming of a woman's voice. Once they heard Vrouw Hansleer splash out into the flooded yard, calling to someone unseen in the darkness:

"Come, Wilhelm! Come and help me move my furniture! Oh, my beautiful furniture! It will all be ruined!"

"Look, woman!" responded the voice. "Dost thou think thou canst save thy wretched furniture in this pass! Thou shalt be thankful to get off with thy life! Take what thou canst carry and be quick, for the Kirk-way is broken through, and the flood will soon be upon us. Hurry, hurry, I say! Merciful St. Anthony! I can hear it roar now!" And true enough, from far in the distance came a faint, ominous sound, low at first as the sighing of a summer breeze, yet dreadful enough to those who understood it to paralyze every muscle with terror. With one final shriek Vrouw Hansleer darted into the house for a moment, then out again, and the children heard the retreating footsteps splashing hurriedly down the road. After that a deathlike silence reigned in the house.

"Gysbert, they have gone and left us!" cried the terrified Jacqueline. "Left us to perish here like rats drowned in a trap when the flood reaches us! Oh, it is cruel, cruel!"

"Nonsense!" retorted her brother. "This is the finest thing that could have happened. I am certain the flood will not rise higher than these windows, so we will be perfectly safe from drowning. And now that they have deserted the house, we can turn our attention to getting out of the door somehow, and not bother with these window bars any longer. I feel certain the wood of the door will yield to this knife, and when we have made a hole big enough, we can crawl out, or burst it open, or pull back the bolts, or something. But we must be quick about it, for we want to get ahead of Dirk and warn the city before October third. That is the day after tomorrow." In the pitchy darkness they groped and found the door. Gysbert began immediately to hack away at one of the panels, finding that it offered much less resistance than did the deeply imbedded iron bars of the window.

"Courage, Jacqueline!" he called at intervals. "We are going to make it soon, without fail. But thou hadst best keep watch at the window." The storm, far from abating, increased in violence. The wind shifted again from the northwest to the southwest, piling up the waters of the German ocean in huge masses and dashing them against the broken dykes. At about eleven o'clock, the ominous, distant murmur increased to a loud roar. Jacqueline at the window called to Gysbert, and together they watched the terrible, awe-inspiring sight, or as much of it as they could see in the darkness.

The dreadful *something* approached nearer and nearer till, with an ear-splitting sound, it suddenly appeared out of the gloom—a huge black wall of water nearly ten feet high, rolling forward with incredible swiftness, deluging, submerging, or pushing before it everything that came in its way. For one horrible instant it surged about the house, rocking the structure to its very foundations and threatening to uproot it outright and fling it to the ground. But the house stood firm, and the vanguard of the flood passed on, leaving the water well up to the second-story window and burying all else in its swirling depths.

When this moment of danger was past, the children breathed again. Gysbert went back to his work on the door with only an, "I told thee so!" while Jacqueline kept watch at her post by the window. The black waters just a little way below her seemed dangerously near, and she imagined them to be rapidly rising. But as they were not yet up to the window, the children were, for the present at least, safe.

At midnight another panorama was spread before their eyes. While Gysbert was digging away at the door, Jacqueline was suddenly startled by a bright flash and a sharp report across the black waste of waters. Instantly it was followed by a resounding roar, as from the mouths of twenty cannon. Gysbert dropped the knife and rushed to the window.

"The fleet! The fleet!" he cried. "They have passed the Kirkway and are making their way toward the city! Long live Admiral Boisot!" It was indeed the doughty admiral and his fearless Beggars of the Sea. Up till that day he had been all but in despair and had even written to the Prince of Orange that the expedition must be abandoned if the wind did not change. Then came the storm. The waters rose, and the Kirk-way, already broken through, was soon leveled, and the flotilla passed in triumph at midnight toward the village of Zoeterwoude. Not half a mile distant from the farmhouse in which the children were incarcerated, the fleet received its first challenge from the guarding Spanish sentinels and answered with such a roar of cannon as all but staggered the astounded outposts.

Then ensued a terrible battle amid a scene perhaps the strangest in which ever a battle was fought. From out the village of Zoeterwoude flocked the Spanish, making their way in any kind of craft on which they could lay hands. The fleet found itself progressing amid half-submerged treetops and orchards, interspersed with chimney stacks and the roofs of low houses. In this strange surrounding they grappled with the Spanish enemy. All the advantage, however, was on their side, as they had but to upset the frail crafts of the Spanish in order to create the most utter rout in the ranks of the enemy.

From the window the children watched the strange spectacle, the room being frequently illuminated by the glare from the cannons. So near were they that even the shouts and cries reached them distinctly, and once was borne to them across the waters the "Song of the Beggars," uplifted in a swelling chorus of triumphant voices:

> *"Long live the Beggars! Wilt thou God's word cherish—*
> *Long live the Beggars! Bold of heart and hand.*
> *Long live the Beggars! God will not see thee perish.*
> *Long live the Beggars! Oh, noble Christian band!"*

Then the fleet swept on, and though the sound of shouting and cannonading diminished but little, the battle passed out of the range of the children's vision.

When morning dawned over the waste of gray waters, it

revealed a weird and desolate scene outside the window. But inside, it lighted up a door in which Gysbert had carved a hole long enough for him to reach his arm through and unloose the bolts!

Chapter XVII

A Crash in the Night

With a mighty effort Gysbert drew back the massive bolt and chain that had so long kept them prisoners, pushed open the demolished door, and they stood outside the room—free at last!

"Go cautiously!" warned he. "We are not yet absolutely sure that everyone is out of the house. But I have this knife, if we meet anyone and it comes to the worst. We won't try to go downstairs—it would be like diving into a tank!" And indeed the water had entered the house and crept three-quarters of the way up the staircase, while bumping against the ceiling of the rooms below floated articles of Vrouw Hansleer's cherished furniture.

From room to room on the second floor the children crept, carefully listening and waiting before they entered any door. But the house was plainly deserted, except for themselves, and in a short time they abandoned all caution, rollicking about in their new freedom like a couple of three-year-olds! Theirs, they soon discovered, were the only other bedrooms on that floor and of course the only ones with barred windows. Two other large apartments occupied the remaining space, one evidently used as a storeroom, the other as a granary. Both had large, open windows through which it would be easy to pass.

For a long time they stood at one of these windows, watching the strange sight outside. The water swept by from the ocean inward with a rapid current, bearing on its surface every imaginable article that could float. Boxes, barrels, furniture of every description, parts of houses, here and there a struggling cow or pig, and not infrequently a great haystack striking out majestically on its impromptu voyage. Once a baby's cradle, completely furnished, came in sight, and Jacqueline went nearly wild with terror and excitement lest it might bear a precious burden in its wrappings. But as it was swept nearer, they saw that it was empty, and both children breathed a sigh of relief.

Meanwhile, Gysbert of the fertile brain had already concocted a plan of escape.

"I tell thee, Jacqueline, we shall get out of here in the easiest way imaginable, if we can only fish out of this muddle the thing we need! Sooner or later some small boat is bound to come along—I know it, for I saw one way off there just now, too far away to reach. First we will try to forage up something to eat, if that is possible, for I am nearly starved and thou must be also. Then we will each station ourselves at a window—I in this room and thou in the granary—to watch for a boat. In this way we can see from both directions. I will be prepared to swim for it if it comes near enough, and then the matter will be simple."

"Aye, but I advise thee to first wash thy face!" responded Jacqueline gaily. "That plague-smitten countenance of thine would frighten away any rescuers we might encounter!" And so, laughing, Gysbert followed her advice, leaning out of the window to dabble his hands in the water that now lapped within a foot of the sill.

Breakfast was about as difficult a matter as any they had to undertake, for everything eatable was downstairs, and it would be worse than useless to attempt procuring anything from those water-soaked depths. Beside, they had very little notion as to the whereabouts of the kitchen. So they turned again to the windows to solve their problem, counting it almost certain that eatables of some sort must in due time go sailing by. Their watch was long but not in vain, for in an hour or so there came in sight a loaf of bread floating so close that it was within reach of a long stick which they used to secure their treasure. Water-logged and unsavory as it was, they devoured it with unspeakable relish, for was it not the first meal they had eaten in freedom this many a weary day!

Then came the watch for the craft that was to bear them away. But the morning wore on, and though they strained their eyes in every direction, nothing in the least available came into view. The water continued to rise till it was only six inches below the window ledge, and should it come much further, their position might be reckoned exceedingly precarious. What they should do if the second floor became flooded except climb out on the roof, they could not imagine. At last, well on in the afternoon, Jacqueline called excitedly from her lookout:

"Gysbert! Gysbert! Come here immediately! The very thing!"

He was at her side in an instant, and there, sure enough, coming rapidly downstream was a little, shallow rowboat bobbing gaily along on the waves. In a very few moments it would be abreast of them.

"I'll have to swim for it," said Gysbert. "It's too far away to reach with the pole!" Hastily flinging off some of his outer garments, he plunged out of the window. He reached the spot opposite the window not an instant too soon; just as the stern of the boat swung by, he grasped it and climbed clumsily aboard. But to Jacqueline's surprise, he did not instantly grasp the oars and start to pull back. Instead he put his hands to his mouth, shouted, "No oars!" and in a twinkling was swept from her sight.

For a moment the situation did not seem very serious, and she waited calmly, thinking he would soon pick up an oar or a pole and return to her. But the time passed on and he did not come. The minutes grew into half an hour, then dragged themselves out to a full hour. Still no Gysbert! Jacqueline became almost distracted, and the situation warranted every fear that thronged her terrified soul. Suppose the water should rise and flood the room? Suppose the night should fall and add its horrors to the prospect? Suppose Dirk Willumhoog should return and snatch her away to unknown terrors? Suppose Gysbert should be swamped in his

little boat and drowned? Suppose?—But the accumulated burden of these fears was too great to be borne. She fell on her knees by the window ledge in an agony of prayer, but could only murmur:
"Oh, God! Help!—"

The afternoon waned and twilight drew down. The water was now within an inch of the window ledge, but Jacqueline did not notice. She knelt with her head buried in her arms and neither saw nor heard anything. Suddenly she was aroused from this half-stupor by a loud shout. She raised her head and perceived to her delight a bulky canal vessel, so close that it looked as though it were about to sail right in the window. Over the prow leaned Gysbert and a man whose face she did not recognize.

"Oh, Jacqueline!" called her brother. "Didst thou think I had forsaken thee? Well, I've had the amazing good fortune to be picked up by Herr Captain Joris Fruytiers, and we came at once to get thee!" It took but a moment to launch the little boat and take Jacqueline on board. As she crept into the boat, Gysbert noticed that the water was just beginning to trickle over the windowsill into the room.

"Jacqueline, we weren't a moment too soon, were we?" he remarked gravely. When the girl had been established in comfortable quarters in the roomy old canal-vessel, Gysbert told her the history of his adventures since he had been swept from her sight. He had at first felt perfectly confident of finding an oar or a pole floating along in the general confusion, so he did not jump out and swim back as he might have done. But the current bore him on and on, and nothing available did he see in all his journey. Presently, as he was watching over one side of the boat, he heard a hearty voice call out from the opposite direction:

"Ship ahoy! Well, if that isn't a pretty small fry commanding that bark!" And he recognized the gruff voice of his former acquaintance on the road to Delft. Captain Fruytiers had lost no time in getting both himself and his little boat aboard the big lugger, which he said he was taking to join the fleet of Boisot at Zwieten. Gysbert quickly told the bluff captain his story and easily persuaded him to turn back and rescue Jacqueline from her perilous position.

This was all, except that from some passing vessel they had picked up the news that the Fleet had made a most triumphant progress all day, scattering the Spaniards right and left as they poured from the captured fortresses and fled along the road to the Hague. But Boisot had now arrived before the strongest Spanish redoubt—the fortress of Lammen, less than five hundred rods from the city. Here he was obliged to halt, for it swarmed with soldiers, bristled with artillery, and defied the fleet to either capture it by force or pass under its guns. The admiral hoped to carry the fort next morning, but he expected a stiff battle.

Joris Fruytiers was to join the rear of the flotilla and help to swell its numbers. Plainly it was no situation for Jacqueline, in the midst of these battle-thirsty Beggars of the Sea, and yet no safer place could be found for her at present. So it was decided that she should remain on board, but Gysbert's head was full of another plan for himself:

"I *must* get into the city somehow! It would be horrible, with relief so near, to have that scoundrel, Dirk, lead in a Spanish regiment and bring about an untimely surrender," he urged. "What is more, I have not a minute to spare, for tomorrow night the deed is to be done. If I can get in tonight, it will be time enough to warn the burgomaster and raise a defending corps to guard the breach. Stay thou here with good Joris Fruytiers, and I will take the small boat and a pair of oars and row to the side where I can get through the scattering army and into Dirk Willumhoog's clever little entrance!"

So Jacqueline acquiesced and watched her brother row away with much trepidation and many muttered prayers for his safety. Darkness soon shut each boat from the sight of the other, but Gysbert paddled on, keeping clear of floating debris as best he could and trying hard to ascertain through the blackness just what was his location. Several times he found himself far out of his course, and thus more than one valuable hour was lost. At length, however, the water became too shallow to continue rowing, and he disembarked, tying the boat to a tree. By several signs he recognized the spot to be near where he had come out of the hidden tunnel several weeks ago. Of the Spanish army at this spot there remained but a few stragglers gathering up their possessions.

Gysbert concluded that the safest place for him was the tree to which he had tied his boat, and he was soon among its branches. From here he watched the departure of the last Spaniard and was just about to descend when one solitary, sneaking shadow attracted his attention. In the blackness of the night he could discover little of its intentions, but as it moved off in the direction of the wall, he decided to get down and follow it. The shadow glided along straight for the wall till it finally disappeared behind the bushes that hid the secret opening. When Gysbert arrived on the spot, there was not even a shadow to be seen. Then a great light dawned on his mind.

"Dirk Willumhoog!" he whispered. "What on earth am I to do now?" For a moment he stood undecided. He dared not venture into the secret passage while his enemy was there. And should Dirk not come back, it was still very unsafe, for he might be guarding the other entrance. But the matter was soon to be solved in a way very different from any he could possibly have imagined.

While he stood considering his course, he was startled by a curious rumbling sound that appeared to emanate from the very earth under his feet. Then there were grinding and groaning noises, low and indistinct, but terrifying beyond imagination. Gysbert's hair fairly rose on his head, and something impelled him to beat the hastiest kind of a retreat. Turning on his heel, he ran with all speed to his boat, unmoored it, pushed it off, and rowed far out upon the black water.

Suddenly there was a terrific sound like an explosion, then a crash that shook the earth for miles around and made Gysbert's little boat rock on the waves till it all but over-turned completely. When the boy recovered himself enough to realize what had happened, it did not take him long to explain the dreadful sounds.

Undermined by the stream so long secretly eating at its base, the whole wall of Leyden between the Cow Gate and the Tower of Burgundy had suddenly fallen in utter ruins!

Chapter XVIII
The Dawn of October Third

Gysbert rowed away frantically from the scene of destruction. He had not, for the moment, the slightest idea what direction he was taking, but his mind was actively at work. The wall of Leyden had fallen in for the space of nearly a quarter of a mile! If the Spaniards had the faintest suspicion of this, he reasoned, they would flock immediately to the scene and make an easy and terrible entrance. There was no defending the breach from the *inside*, for the brave but hunger-enfeebled corps of John Van der Does would be as nothing before the fierce thousands of the Spanish army. To his mind there remained but one course—he must in some way get word to Admiral Boisot and his Sea Beggars and let them make an entrance into the city before the Spaniards got wind of the disaster.

With this end in view he looked about him, ascertained as nearly as he could the position of the fleet, and commenced to row steadily in that direction. As he drew near the Fortress of Lammen, however, he became aware that something very strange was taking place. Wonderingly he shipped his oars and turned about to watch the curious sight. Myriads of tiny lights twinkled across the dark waste of waters. There was almost no sound, but only a vague impression that something mysterious was happening. After a time the lights formed themselves into a long procession which seemed to flit steadily across the one remaining causeway that led to the Hague.

The boy sat breathless, eager, marveling at this apparently never-ending procession of lights, twinkling in single file over what seemed the very face of the water. For a time he could find no explanation for this singular spectacle, till all at once the truth flashed on him. The Spaniards were retreating! Under cover of darkness, they were silently sneaking away, fleeing panic-stricken from the unknown terror of that hideous sound in the night—fleeing like cowards at the very moment when fortune had rendered their entrance to the coveted city as easy as stepping over a log!

Truly had God's providence operated in a marvelous manner! At the crash of the falling wall, the terrified citizens of Leyden believed that the Spaniards had at last effected their entrance in some horrible way. The Spanish, on the other hand, felt certain that the citizens were making a final, desperate sortie. And between this new danger on one side and the fierce Sea Beggars and the inward-surging ocean on the other, they deemed retreat to be their only course, short of complete extermination, and they fled away in the night.

For two hours Gysbert sat in his little boat and watched the retreat. In all the city of Leyden or its environments, he was the only soul that night who was aware of the true state of affairs. At length the last few straggling lights disappeared, and all was silence and darkness. When he was convinced that a nearer approach was safe, he rowed slowly toward Fort Lammen, reconnoitering carefully at almost every yard. But the nearer he drew, the plainer it became that the fort was absolutely deserted. Boldly landing at the foot of the battlement, he entered at the cannon-defended gate and found the enclosure empty. Colonel Borgia and his troops had fled so hastily that even some of their time-honored battle flags were left behind!

Gysbert was not content, however, with ascertaining only the condition of Lammen. It was quite possible that the retreating army had halted at Leyderdorp, the headquarters of Valdez, half a mile away. Now that he was about it, he concluded that he might as well investigate there before daylight. Again pushing off his boat, he paddled across the shallow lake that now spread over what was ordinarily meadow-land. But Leyderdorp was also deserted. Guided by a dying campfire, he reached a small building which he guessed to be the abode of General Valdez. The fire was built before the doorway, and over it was still cooking a pot of "hodge-podge," or stewed meat and vegetables. Evidently it had been intended for the breakfast of the general, but so speedy had been the retreat that it was left behind in the hurry.

"Whew!" ejaculated Gysbert, leaning over the pot. "This smells right savory to a stomach that has had nothing today but half a water-soaked loaf! Thanks, my cowardly friends! I'll partake of your bounty before I do another thing!" Swinging the pot from its hook and scarcely waiting for it to cool, he helped himself to a large quantity doled out with a great iron spoon and ate as only a half-starved, healthy boy can eat, till he could hold no more.

Hunger satisfied, he proceeded to investigate the fleeing general's quarters. By the dying firelight he could discern several maps of Leyden and the outlying districts pinned about the walls, and on the table lay a scrap of paper hastily written upon. Gysbert took it out to the fire, coaxed the embers into a blaze, and, kneeling over the flames, tried to decipher the writing. It was in Latin, and very poor Latin at that, and was plainly the general's farewell to the city. Gysbert had been for over a year studying this language in school, so he was able to construe its meaning fairly well.

"*Vale civitas!*" he read. "*Valete castelli parvii, qui relicti estis propter aquam et non per vim inimicorum!*"

"'*Vale civitas!*'—That's 'Farewell city of Leyden!' I suppose. '*Valete castelli parvii—*' What in the world can he mean by that! If I had written such stuff in the Latin school, the master would have boxed my ears and kept me in from play for three days to write my conjugations! What this doughty Spaniard *wished* to remark was probably, 'Farewell miserable town! Thou art abandoned because of the water, and not because of the strength of thy resistance!' Oh, ho! Noble Valdez, thy Latin is as poor as thy courage! I must keep this carefully to hand to Admiral Boisot."

But the dawn was already breaking, and Gysbert hurried back to Lammen, carrying with him as a souvenir the iron pot of hodge-podge. Early that morning there was to be a combined assault on the fort by the admiral's fleet and the citizens of the town. The day before, Boisot had dispatched the last pigeon into the city, urging the starving populace to aid him in one last, desperate attack. With the first streaks of daylight, all was in readiness, and the admiral prepared to push his fleet under the very guns of cannon-bristling Lammen. But to his great astonishment, as the flotilla drew nearer, not a sound came from within the fort, not a vestige of life was to be seen anywhere. A sickening fear assailed him that the Spaniards had entered the walls during the night, which would explain the hideous sounds he had heard, and were already sacking the city.

Suddenly upon the summit of the breastwork appeared the figure of a small boy. With one hand he waved his cap, and in the other he brandished a great pot of hodge-podge.

"Come on! Come on!" he shouted. "They've gone! They fled in the night! Have no fear!" For a moment good Boisot could hardly believe his senses. But his sailors lost no time; they pushed the fleet to the very walls of the fortress and found it to be true. Past the terrible Lammen they floated in triumph. The watching, wondering citizens of the city opened the gates with shouts of joy, and the conquering fleet sailed in. Leyden was saved!

In the twinkling of an eye were the canals and docks lined with throngs of the starving populace. They grasped with famished delight the loaves of bread thrown to them by the jolly Beggars of the Sea and nearly choked themselves to death trying to swallow huge mouthfuls without even chewing them.

Gysbert waited impatiently on the fortress till he saw the familiar lugger of Joris Fruytiers come into view and then ran down and climbed aboard her. Words cannot describe the meeting between himself and Jacqueline, who during that night of terror and uncertainty had given him up for dead. They had much to tell each other but little time to give to it, for old Captain Joris demanded at once the whole history of Gysbert's night and was loud in the praise of his bravery.

When the last vessel had entered the gates, staunch Admiral Boisot stood on the deck of his flagship and made a speech to the assembled crowds. He ended by saying that both the city and the Sea Beggars had much to thank God for and proposed that they all proceed to the great cathedral of St. Peter to render their praise to the God of Battles at once. Then many remembered what in the excitement of the moment they had quite forgotten—that the day was Sunday! With the admiral at their head, they marched in solid ranks down the Breede Straat and entered the cathedral reverently.

"Shall we go?" questioned Gysbert of his sister. "Or dost thou think we had best go straight home first?"

"No," answered Jacqueline, "I think God's worship claims us before all else!" And they entered the church with the rest. Only a suffering, plague-stricken, lately besieged and recently delivered people could have rendered such thanks as rose up to God's throne from St. Peter's that day. There were sounds of suppressed sobbing all through the congregation, and strong men's eyes grew moist when the clergyman read:

"'Oh, that men would praise the Lord for his goodness, and for His wonderful works to the children of men!

"'They cried unto the Lord in their trouble, and He saved them out of their distresses!

"'For He satisfieth the longing soul, and filleth the hungry with good things!

"'He brought them out of darkness and the shadow of death. He brake their bands in sunder!

"'For He commandeth and raiseth the stormy wind which lifteth up the waves!

"'Oh, give thanks unto the Lord, for He is good, for His mercy endureth forever!'"

Then the congregation rose, and every voice joined in their battle hymn:

"A mighty fortress is our God,
A bulwark never failing!
Our helper He amid the flood
Of mortal ills prevailing.
For still our ancient foe
Doth seek to work us woe,
His craft and power are great,
And armed with cruel hate—
On earth is not his equal!"

But in the midst of the second verse, a general emotion checked the volume of sound. One by one the voices failed, till at last the whole vast multitude broke down and wept like children out of the great thankfulness for their deliverance. In their corner by a window, Gysbert openly sobbed with his head on his arm, and Jacqueline stood with the tears raining down her face and the glad light of happiness in her eyes.

"Come," she said when the service was over. "We must hasten at once to Vrouw Voorhaas! I have sad misgivings that all is not well with her." They had, however, gone but a few steps when they heard a shout behind them, and, turning, they beheld Dr. Pieter de Witt beckoning to them and running as fast as he could come. Seizing Gysbert, he hugged him distractedly, and he squeezed Jacqueline's hand till she almost screamed aloud.

"You blessed, blessed children!" he shouted. "I never supposed I should see you again! Ah, this will indeed reanimate old Jan, and even Vrouw Voorhaas may—but come!" And he rushed them along so fast that Jacqueline could hardly find breath in which to ask after the sick woman.

"She is very, very low!" panted De Witt. "We hardly expect her to live through the day, but the sight of you two may make some difference—I cannot tell! Hurry, hurry!" They reached Belfry Lane, stopped a moment to regain breath, and all three crept upstairs as softly as possible. The opened door revealed a strange sight to their astonished gaze. Jan stood huddled in a corner, eyes wide with amazement, apprehension, and doubt. Vrouw Voorhaas, withered and shrunken by her long illness, half sat up in her bed, looking more like a ghost than a living being. But most astonishing of all, over her leaned a stranger, a tall, gaunt man clad in the uniform of the Beggars of the Sea. He bent over the woman, clasping her hand and questioning her anxiously in a low voice. Her face was lined with despair, and her words, though faint, were audible to the listeners at the door:

"Gone!—gone!—not here!—" Suddenly she raised her head and saw the newcomers. With a great happy cry she pointed to them:

"They are here! They are safe!—I have fulfilled my duty—praise God!" And she fell back unconscious on the pillow.

Chapter XIX

The Secret Out

Dr. de Witt flew to Vrouw Voorhaas's assistance, pushing the stranger unceremoniously aside in his haste. For a moment no one spoke while he busied himself over the sick woman. Then he turned to the intruder, sternly inquiring:

"Who art thou, and why art thou here?" The man pulled off his cap ornamented with the Beggar's crescent and drew himself up to face the physician.

"I am Dr. Cornellisen," he said, "and I have come to claim my children!"

Struck dumb with amazement and incredulity, not a soul moved. Then De Witt advanced a step and stuttered:

"But—b-b-but—Dr. Cornellisen is dead!"

"No, he is not dead!" answered the stranger. "He never died—but there was excellent reason why he should be considered so. Come, children! Will you not kiss your father?" And he held out his arms to the two. Then the spell was broken. Doubting no longer, Jacqueline and Gysbert rushed into his embrace, while Jan blubbered in his joy like a great baby and Dr. de Witt tore around the room, alternately laughing and crying and trying to shake hands with Jan. The confusion lasted many minutes, during which time Vrouw Voorhaas came unassisted to her senses and smiled understandingly on the scene.

"Oh, my boy and girl!" said the father at last. "God has brought us through many strange trials and vicissitudes to the happiness of this meeting! But now, if it pleases Him, we shall never part again."

"But Father," answered Jacqueline, "we can scarcely yet realize that thou art our father, so much dost thou seem like one risen from the dead! Wilt thou not tell us the whole story?"

"I will indeed, daughter, and right here and now, since it must seem passing strange to you all." They sat down to listen breathlessly while Dr. Cornellisen began his story. As the tale unfolded, it revealed many things to them that had long been hidden in mystery.

"Jacqueline here must remember," he commenced, "the time when I mysteriously disappeared six years ago. And so must thou, Dr. de Witt, for now I recognize thy face and thank thee for thy devotion to me and mine. Well, as you all know, the young Count de Buren was cunningly enticed away from the University of Louvain by King Philip's orders, to be taken to Spain and either killed outright or kept as a hostage. He was only a boy of thirteen, and they flattered and cajoled him with fine promises. Count de Chassy had been sent from Spain with a retinue under the pretext of escorting the young count on a visit to His Majesty Philip II.

"The boy was under my special care, and I counseled him strongly not to accept these doubtful honors. But the child was uncontrollable in his desire to have his own way, and before I could get word to the Prince of Orange, the start was made. Young De Buren was to travel in state, though secretly. He had a retinue of two pages, two valets, a cook and an accountant, and moreover insisted that I should go with him as a personal companion. I was nothing loath to do so, for I thought I might thus be able to shield him from harm. My presence, however, was not relished by the Spanish envoys, but at first they thought it best not to oppose the boy's wish.

"We reached the borders of Spain and camped one night in a little mountain village. As the evening was fine, I determined to take a short stroll before retiring. On reaching a lonely spot, I was set upon by a masked man, overpowered, stabbed in the ribs, dragged into the bushes and left for dead. I know now that my assailant was Dirk Willumhoog and that he had been hired to kill me!" At this familiar name the children gasped.

"Next morning the cavalcade passed on without me, telling the boy I had left in the night to return to Louvain. But Dirk's thrust had not quite reached its mark! I was picked up next day by some kindhearted peasants, carefully tended for weeks, and at last was as well as ever. I was, of course, perfectly unknown to them and remained so. In the meantime, I had decided on a plan. I communicated with Vrouw Voorhaas and told her to sell the house, take you children and go to live in Leyden. She was to carefully conceal the fact that I was alive and bring you children up in her good care till I should return. I knew that you would be more than safe in her excellent keeping, but I never dreamed that my term of absence would be so long.

"At the same time I wrote to the Prince of Orange, who was almost distracted for the safety of his son. I told him what had happened and also that I intended to disguise myself as a Dutch malcontent or Glipper under the name of Dr. Leonidus Graafzoon and obtain entrance to the court of Spain. There I could remain for a time and watch over the fortunes of the young boy, so cruelly enticed into the midst of his father's enemies. The Prince wrote back that by so doing I would earn his eternal gratitude and procured me letters of introduction to the Spanish court, under my assumed name.

"There I remained for five years, carefully guarding the safety of the count. At the end of that time, however, it became apparent that they contemplated no harm toward young De Buren. He was systematically well-treated, carefully educated, and seemed rather to like his new surroundings than otherwise. I had, of course, been most anxious to be reunited with my family and begged the Prince to free me from my duties and allow me to join you. He gave a hearty and gracious consent, and I began my preparations to return to Leyden when the news of the siege reached me, and I knew that great and imminent danger threatened you. I left Spain, as I learned later, not a day too soon, for my old enemy Dirk Willumhoog had in some way discovered my secret, unearthed all my past history, and was hot upon a little scheme of his own.

"Vrouw Voorhaas sent me word—it was the last I heard from her—that a man whom she described as Dirk called on her one day when you both were out, informed her that he knew her secret and who you children were and all about me. Then he tried to bribe her to give you up to him, offering a good round sum in gold. When she refused, he threatened to get possession of you in some other way. She was wild with anxiety for your safety and begged me to hasten to Leyden without delay. But by the time I reached Holland, the siege was in full progress, and all thought of access to the city was hopeless. Having thus a double reason for serving the city, I went to Zeeland and joined the Sea Beggars. I fought all the way to Leyden on the *Ark of Delft* and have been frequently almost prostrated by the alternations of hope and despair. But I am here, we are reunited—and now you know my story!"

"Yes," said Jacqueline with a long-drawn breath, "but I still do not see why Dirk wished to get possession of Gysbert and myself."

"Why! Dost thou not comprehend!—" interrupted the boy. "He wanted to hold us for a ransom, well knowing Father would pay any price to have us back. Dost thou not remember how we overheard him telling Vrouw Hansleer that we would surely mean more money to them? And that is why they were so careful of us too!"

"Yes," said Dr. Cornellisen, "that is what he wanted with you. But now I must hear your story too. How came Vrouw Voorhaas to think she had lost you?" The children recounted their adventures, first one and then the other interrupting in a breathless, excited fashion. At last Gysbert ended with the recital of the singular adventure of the night before and the terrible falling of the wall just after Dirk Willumhoog had entered the breach.

"It doubtless became his tomb," remarked Dr. Cornellisen thoughtfully, "and a terrible ending indeed—too terrible to linger over!"

"No, no!" interrupted old Jan eagerly. "It was but just—just!

Was he not about to betray the city for filthy Spanish gold, and does it not fulfill every word of that verse from the Scriptures—'In the snare which the wicked hath set is his own foot taken!'"

"The Bible says also—'Judge not that ye be not judged,'" said Dr. Cornellisen quietly. "So we will leave Dirk Willumhoog forever, as he has gone to face his sentence in a higher court than any human one."

Presently Dr. de Witt made a sign to old Jan, and the two crept quietly out together, leaving the happy family alone for a while in their new joy of glad reunion.

Chapter XX

The Great Day

Four months had passed since the lifting of the great siege of Leyden. No sooner had the Spaniards effected their retreat than the gales shifted, the wind changed to the east, and the sea retreated and left the waters to drain from the sodden, half-drowned fields. In due time the work of reconstructing the dykes commenced, and the exhausted city once more lifted up its head, smiling to meet its renewal of life.

No one rejoiced more over the wonderful victory than did the Prince of Orange. And to express his gratitude to the citizens for their enduring heroism during all the long, weary months, he determined to present the city with a gift. This gift was one more highly valued by the Dutch than anything else it was in his power to bestow, for it was neither more nor less than a *university*.

Accordingly, the University of Leyden, destined in after years to be so illustrious, was endowed with a rich sum of money and provided with professors and instructors, the most learned and distinguished in all the Netherlands. Among these was Dr. Cornellisen, whose valuable personal services the Prince was never weary of praising. William of Orange declared that a professorship was all too poor a reward for such devotion, but the doctor would accept of no other, vowing that his ambition was completely satisfied in being connected with such a wonderful institution of learning.

On the fifth of February, 1575, all preparations being completed, the solemn ceremony of consecrating the university was to take place. It was to be a great day, and the whole city was on tiptoe of expectation in consequence. The weather was perfect, and even though so early in the year, the atmosphere had a spring-like flavor. The canals were packed with gay barges, houses flaunted in bunting and floral decorations, and a festive air was prevalent in every quarter of the city. At seven o'clock in the morning there was a solemn ceremony of consecration in the great church of St. Peter. Jacqueline and Gysbert could not but think of another scene in this same church only four months before—but how different! There was no weeping now! All the new professors filed in and took their places in the chancel, looking very grand and imposing in their flowing robes and decorations.

"Look, look, Vrouw Voorhaas! There is Father!" whispered Gysbert, pulling her sleeve. And the faithful woman, now quite recovered from her long illness, nodded and smiled approvingly. The impressive service continued, ending with the singing of the famous hymn—"A Mighty Fortress Is Our God!" But this time the joyful anthem was interrupted by no sobs of overwrought emotion as on that memorable Sunday when Leyden was saved.

Then came a gorgeous procession. Up the wide Breede Straat it moved slowly and majestically under great triumphal arches and over pavements strewn with flowers. First there was a grand military escort in which Adrian Van der Werf, the brave and loyal burgomaster, rode at the head of his company of burgher guards. This was followed by glittering chariots and wonderfully arrayed figures representing Justice, Peace, the four Gospels, and many mythological and allegorical characters. But in the midst of these there was a little break, and then appeared, riding on a milk-white horse, a fair young girl. Her beautiful, golden hair floated all about her, she was clothed in a long, trailing robe of white silk, and on one shoulder sat a glistening pigeon, fastened to her by a small golden chain. She represented *Medicine* and carried a garland of healing herbs in one hand. As she passed through the crowds, a great cry went up—"Jacqueline! Jacqueline of the Carrier Pigeons!"

For all recognized her as the sweet, unselfish girl who had done and risked so much in the terrible days of the plague and siege, and not a few were also acquainted with the remarkable story of her father's return.

It was a proud moment in her life, but she bore herself with the ease of entire unconsciousness, for her thoughts were on the honor of the university and not on herself. Last in the procession came the professors and instructors, and the whole passed through every prominent street of the city till it came to the cloister of Saint Barbara, the place prepared for the new university. Here there was a long address by the Reverend Casper Kolhas, orator of the day, and later on a magnificent banquet. It was nightfall before all was over and the tired participants returned to their various homes.

In a fine, roomy house on the Marendorfstrasse, the new quarters of the Cornellisen family, Gysbert and Jacqueline waited to bid their father goodnight. When his social duties at last permitted him to come to the children, he entered the room and they gathered about him to talk it all over before going to bed.

"I am proud of my children!" said Dr. Cornellisen. "Proud of thee, Jacqueline, because thou hast borne thyself with so much grace and dignity during a difficult day. Proud of thee, Gysbert, because thou didst not complain of having no prominent part in the parade, although thy services to the city during the siege were really most praiseworthy. And now I am going to tell thee that the Prince wished me to allow thee to ride on a float all by thyself, dressed as thou wert on the morning of October third, with the pot of hodge-podge at thy side!" Gysbert's eyes opened wide at this.

"But I would not permit it," went on his father. "Thou art yet too young to take so prominent a part, and I did not think it best for thee. But to make up for this, I am going to allow thee, in addition to studying in the university, to take a course in art under the very finest master that can be procured. Does that please thee, son?"

"Father, Father!" answered the boy, and his voice trembled

with the intensity of his feeling. "I know naught in all this world that would please me so much!"

"And as for thee, Jacqueline," said the doctor, turning to her, "since thou hast shown thyself so proficient in the healing art—and Dr. de Witt tells me thou didst do wonders during the plague—I shall give thee a special course under my own tuition in the university. Thou mayst not ever become a titled physician, that not being exactly a woman's work, but at least thou shalt have all the understanding of one. Daughter, I trust that makes thee happy." Jacqueline did not answer in words, but she put her arms about his neck and laid her soft cheek against his own, and her father understood.

"And now let us call in Vrouw Voorhaas and Jan," cried Gysbert, "and tell them the good news!" Vrouw Voorhaas expressed her approval in her own quiet way, and Jan, who now occupied a trusted position in the household, shouted hurrah like a boy! In the midst of this rejoicing, Dr. de Witt dropped in on his way home from the burgomaster's.

"And let me tell you all something else," he added when he had been informed of the children's good fortune. "Mynheer Van der Werf has been commissioned by the Prince, in the name of the city, to buy all thy carrier pigeons, Juffrouw Jacqueline, that were used during the siege, preserve them carefully while they live, and have them stuffed and placed in the Leyden Museum when they die. Likewise he undertakes to buy thy hodge-podge pot, Gysbert, for a good round sum, and place that also in the museum. So I suppose you will both have to make up your minds to part with these cherished possessions."

"I'm only too glad to part with mine," said Gysbert, "for I shall be proud to go and look at that old iron pot in its honored place in the museum and think how I found it that horrible night and how good the Spanish hodge-podge tasted that I got out of it!"

"And I," said Jacqueline, "will give up my pigeons since the Prince wishes it, but I think I will keep 'William of Orange' for myself. He rode with me in the procession today, and I love him both for the name he bears and the part he played in those dreadful days. No, I am sure I cannot part with my faithful 'William of Orange!'"

***

But the future was to hold one more *great day* for the Cornellisen family, at which we must have one glimpse before we leave them.

Five years more had passed, and again it was October third, the anniversary of the great Relief of Leyden. The day was always set apart as one of feasting and general thanksgiving, and a holiday air pervaded the city. But in the Cornellisen home were preparations of quite another character—for it was the wedding day of Jacqueline. Grown into a fair and noble womanhood was this same Jacqueline of splendid promise, who had so bravely discharged what seemed to her the highest duty in the days of the memorable siege. She was going to marry loyal, true-hearted Pieter de Witt, who had learned to love her in the terrible days when they tended the starving and plague-stricken together. Patiently had he waited and watched her grow to be a sweet, unselfish woman. Then he had courted and won her, and tonight she stood ready to become his wife.

No prettier bride could have possibly been imagined than Jacqueline as she stood robed in her wedding garments. Vrouw Voorhaas hovered over her lovingly, giving the last tender, anxious touches to the array of her beloved charge. Presently the door opened, and Gysbert laughingly demanded admission—Gysbert no longer a little lad of fourteen, but a tall, fine youth of nineteen. He entered at his sister's bidding and surveyed her admiringly from top to toe.

"Thou art perfect, my Jacqueline, but no one knows how I hate to part with thee, even to Pieter, whom I do certainly love."

"But thou art not parting with me, Gysbert. Are we not going to stay right here with thee and Father? I shall be with thee as much as ever!"

"Well, I suppose that is true. After all, I am only gaining a brother by this! But dost thou remember, Jacqueline, how we used to talk over our ambitions up there on Hengist Hill? I am in a fair way to gain mine, for what dost thou think!—Karel Van Mander told Father that I bid fair to become a great artist if I persevere, and he is the greatest himself in the Netherlands at the present time! And then the Prince of Orange admired and purchased my last picture and has promised to hang it in his salon in the *Prinsenhof*. But what of *thy* great ambition, sister?"

"Ah!" she answered laughingly. "I have studied medicine till I have it at my finger ends. I am the daughter of one physician and am about to become the wife of another! What more can I ask? I am content, Gysbert!"

"But is it not splendid," said the boy, "that the Prince is to be present at the wedding! Thou art much honored, Jacqueline, and I am wild to see him again. He is still my hero and ideal!"

"Thou hast not yet seen the present he sent," added Jacqueline. "It came but a short time ago. Look!" She held out her arm and exhibited a beautiful bracelet set with many pearls. In the center was a small gold plate on which was engraved:

<blockquote>
To Jacqueline of the Carrier Pigeons
from
William of Orange-Nassau,
In memory of faithful services in Leyden,
1574
</blockquote>

"I prize this more than aught else I received!" she said softly.

Then in came Jan, brave in wedding finery, to have a last intimate view of his Jacqueline. Round and round her he walked, speechless with admiration, and could only smile and chuckle and rub his hands and stroke her dainty garments with half-shy, half-reverent touches. Last of all came her father in his scholarly robes of the university and took her in his arms for a final caress.

"Thou art sweet and fair, my darling!" he whispered. "Be as good a wife to Pieter as thou hast been ever a daughter to me, and Heaven itself could ask no more! But come! The Prince and his suite have arrived, the guests are all assembled, and thy future husband waits to claim thee!"

And so, to the sound of merry wedding music, we say farewell to Jacqueline of the Carrier Pigeons!

The End